THE
Purest Love
FOR THE
COLDEST
THUG
2

A NOVEL BY
MISS JENESEQUA

Who knew the purest love would turn out to be the most addictive substance?

Kisan Williams knew from the second he laid eyes on So/ána Winters that he wanted her. But from wanting her to now loving her was something that he never expected to happen. And now that it has, Kisan is torn. Should he make things work with the woman he loves or stay with the woman who birthed his precious daughter?

So/ána Winters is still distraught from Kisan's sudden end to their relationship. She knows she loves him and doesn't want to be without him. Despite her mind telling her to forget all about him, her heart yearns for his presence. Will her determination result in her taking control and going full force for the man she wants, regardless of his decision for them to be apart? Or will she fall into the arms of another?

There's a big secret lurking, and it could send Kisan into a state of pure hatred. And that ice-cold heart that was once melted by So/ána could instantly freeze into an ice-cold box. In the second installment of The Purest Love for The Coldest Thug, lines will be crossed, tears will be shed, and love will endure. But can everyone survive the conflicting times ahead, or will the conflict get the best of them?

ACKNOWLEDGMENTS

For Jahquel: In this industry, you never know who you can truly trust. But I know for a fact that I can always count on you. You're a real one! Thank you for your advice and always cheering your girl up. I love you!

For PMoney aka Porscha Sterling: I absolutely loveeeee you, P! You know how much I do! I appreciate all that you've done for me and all that you continue to do for me. Thank you so much for everything. #RoyaltyForever.

For Brie Tolbert & Laticia Green: Both of you drive me absolutely crazy, but I wouldn't have it any other way! You're both so hilarious, and I'm grateful to have amazing readers like you. Thank you for always making my day.

"Hood niggas are typically cold motherfuckers.
So melting one? Now that's rare. Rare and *pure*."

— JOSEPHINE JENESEQUA

PREVIOUSLY IN THE PUREST LOVE FOR THE COLDEST THUG...

*H*er eyes fluttered open only to see Khaleeq placing his clothes on his body. She sat up on her bed and observed as he quickly got dressed. Sensing the sudden movement behind him, Khaleeq turned around to face her just as he placed his shirt over his head. Monalisa gave him a weak smile, but he didn't smile back. And him failing to smile back reminded her how much of a mistake last night had been. A big mistake. Khaleeq placed his watch on his wrist before intensely looking into her eyes.

"Monalisa... what happened last night..." *Was amazing, magical, and a night like no other,* she mused to herself. "...can't happen ever again."

Even though Monalisa knew that he was right, an uneasy sensation formed in her heart. She nodded in agreement without saying anything. Khaleeq then gave her one last look before taking his leave.

As much as Monalisa knew she was going to regret it, she needed to call April and tell her she could no longer be her wedding planner. There was no way she could do the job after what she had done. *But how will I get out of this? And after all she's been through with her other wedding planner, are you sure you want to crush her spirit? Because that's exactly what you'll do if you quit, Monalisa.* Her conflicted thoughts continued to spin in her head while she reached over to her lamp stand to grab her phone, only for her phone to vibrate in her palm.

Zing!

She looked down to see the incoming text message from her sister in their group chat.

Solána: *Kisan and I slept together. Then after he said it was all a mistake.*

Then Sabrina's text message came in.

Sabrina: *I cheated on Kadeem with... Troy.*

Sabrina: *Kadeem walked in on us.*

Sabrina: *He almost killed us both when he lifted his gun at us. He didn't shoot though. He just walked out, staring at me like I was nothing to him.*

Sabrina: *I want to die.*

Monalisa couldn't believe it. Her sisters were going through it, and as much as she wanted to confide in them about what happened between her and Khaleeq last night, she just couldn't do it. She now had to put her own personal drama aside and come to the rescue of her sisters.

"You need to tell them before he does."

Glancing across the kitchen table and seeing her best friend, Ruby, give her a grim look told Carolina all she needed to know. This wasn't a game.

"I can't."

"Carolina, you have to."

The past wasn't something that she liked to bring up too much. Things were just better when you didn't have to dig up old secrets. However, someone had come back into Carolina's life determined to release all past secrets.

"You can't stop him from telling them, as he already knows where they live. It's better for you to tell them than a complete stranger."

"But how do I tell them without them hating me?"

"You just have to be frank with them," Ruby advised. "There's no other way out of it. I know it isn't easy, but the girls deserve to know the truth, and they deserve to hear it from you."

Carolina didn't want to do this. She knew that revealing to the girls her secret would turn everything upside down. The beautiful, trusting relationship she had with them would crumble in seconds. But it seemed like she had no choice on the matter. The girls either found out from her or found out from someone else.

~

"YOU STILL HAVEN'T SWITCHED *on your phone and told him where you are?"*

April shook her head 'no' with satisfaction. *"I don't want him to know where I am right now. But I'll probably go back home today,"* April revealed *while sipping on her brandy. "Thank you for giving me a place to stay though."*

"No worries, girl," Dazhanae replied, *filling her glass with more brandy. "You know I got you."*

After her argument with Khaleeq, April needed to escape to a place she knew he wouldn't find her. And that place was Dazhanae's secret condo located in North Miami. It was a secret because Kisan didn't know about it. If Kisan didn't know about it, then none of The Williams knew about it, which meant that April could feel secure enough staying here without Khaleeq bursting in and demanding for her to come home.

The two friends were relaxing on Dazhanae's couches while drinking and talking. It felt good for Dazhanae to be able to let her hair down without having to worry about Luciana. Since Kisan was around much more often, she had more time for herself. She had told Kisan she was going to visit her mom, not wanting him to know that she was with April, because if he had found out, then Khaleeq would find out.

"How's things now that Kisan's around more?"

"Great. I really can't complain," Dazhanae admitted with a pleased smile. *"I have more time to myself these days, and it's nice. I think Kisan seeing Luciana so unwell was a real wake up call for him. It's nice to have him around much more. And of course, it's nice to fall asleep in his arms."*

"A.K.A. it's nice to get that dick on demand whenever you want it," April blurted out, *making the both of them laugh wildly.*

"I mean, I'm not complaining, like I said," Dazhanae commented with a sneaky grin and taking more sips from her brandy.

"Course you're not, bitch. Khaleeq's a beast in the sheets, so I expect nothing less from the oldest Williams."

"Yeah, you're definitely right about that," Dazhanae agreed. "He's even more aggressive than usual."

"You mean rough?"

"Yeah. I mean, he's always been quite aggressive in the bedroom, but these days, I feel more anger from him more than anything else."

"Really? What's he angry about?"

"I really don't know," Dazhanae replied with a shrug. "But I do need to find out, because it's starting to affect me."

"Affect you how?" April asked as she drank her alcohol.

"I hardly cum."

April almost choked on her drink and quickly started coughing.

"It's bad. I know," Dazhanae spoke up for her.

"Bad? Girl, that's horrible. You definitely need to get to the bottom of that. I could never imagine not climaxing with Khaleeq. Like ever."

"Lucky for some," Dazhanae muttered with envy before lifting her cup to her lips.

"That would be like... be like a sin. I can't even imagine it." April laughed wildly, her liquor clearly getting to her head. "The only thing tempting me to go back home to him right now is so that I can get some dick."

"I'm surprised you've lasted a whole night without it, 'cause I know how much you love that dick."

"Indeed, girl, indeed." April gulped down the rest of her drink before reaching across the coffee table for the brandy bottle and refilling her cup. "After this wedding, my main goal is to have a baby."

"Already, girl? You sure you ready for a kid so soon after marriage?"

"Yesss." She giggled lightly, sipping more of her drink. "I want one so bad. They're so cute and little. I want a mini me."

"Well, yeah, they're cute, but girl, they're a lot. Luciana was a trouble-maker when she was much littler."

"But you still love her so much, and you're even lucky because she looks nothing like Kisan and everything like you. Don't you want another one?"

"Not right now." Dazhanae drank some more of her brandy before changing her words. "Actually, with how much time Kisan spends around these days, I kinda do want another baby."

"To be fair, Luciana's only four, making her still a baby."

"True," Dazhanae agreed. "But seeing Kisan spend so much time with her kinda makes me feel guilty these days. Especially when he hasn't got a child of his own."

April suddenly cackled at Dazhanae. "Yeah, girl, I can definitely tell that liquor's gotten to you. Luciana is Kisan's child, silly."

Dazhanae chugged the rest of her brandy down her throat before smiling and giggling lightly. "Luciana isn't his child, girl."

April gave her a crazy look, clearly thinking that she was out of her mind right now. But when she continued speaking, April wasn't so sure if it was just the liquor making Dazhanae say wild things.

"Her real father is his best friend, Lucas. We messed around four years ago when Kisan and I briefly broke up, and he got me pregnant, not Kisan. But the sad part is, none of them know the truth. I've just been stringing Kisan along for the past few years, allowing him to believe that he's Luciana's father when he's not. Girl, I even named her after Lucas."

CHAPTER 1

*D*azhanae had slept like a baby. The ladies had stayed in the living room, drinking away before Dazhanae had dozed off, but April hadn't been able to sleep all night. The shock from Dazhanae's words were still within her. Drunk or not, Dazhanae had revealed truths that she hadn't wished to, and April wasn't sure she could look at her friend in the same way anymore.

Now here she stood, watching her reflection in the bathroom mirror only to see a stressed look engraved deep into her face. Her plan had been to go home to Khaleeq last night, but drinking had gotten the best of her, and the shock from Dazhanae's words wouldn't allow her to go anywhere. But her new plan was to head back home to Khaleeq this morning.

The only thing was, she wasn't sure how she was supposed to look at Khaleeq, knowing this grave secret. They never kept secrets from each other, so this one right here was going to be the first.

Truthfully, April wanted to run home to Khaleeq and spill what Dazhanae had revealed last night, but the other part of her wanted to act like last night hadn't happened. What was she going t—

Knock! Knock!

"April."

April's head instantly turned to face the bathroom door. Her attention now alert to the woman on the other side of the door.

"Yeah?"

"I just wanted to check up on you, girl," Dazhanae announced in a concerned tone. "We had way too much to drink last night."

"Yeah," April said with an awkward laugh. "We did."

"Way too much... and I have a feeling that I said a lot of bullshit last night. A lot of bullshit that wasn't true."

April swallowed hard and remained silent, not sure what to say in return to her words. Hearing Dazhanae try to play off what she had said last night didn't change how April felt about the situation.

"April?"

"Yeah?"

"You hear what I said?"

"Yeah, girl, I heard you," April responded coolly. "Sure did."

"Alright, great. I take it you're heading back to Khaleeq now?"

"Yeah."

April still undeniably had her doubts and worries about Dazhanae's words from last night. She basically admitted to playing Kisan by stating that Luciana wasn't his child. Her father was Kisan's best friend, Lucas. But the only thing bothering her was telling Khaleeq the truth. She didn't want to keep this away from Khaleeq, but she didn't want to be the catalyst to a terrible fire.

"So... he walked in on us... and... and..."

Sabrina could feel the tears sliding down her cheeks as she tried to speak up to her sisters. She struggled to look them in the eyes. The embarrassment and shame that she felt was out of this world. She still couldn't believe what had went down.

Sabrina slowly pulled open her front door and was greeted to his attractive face. Even after all this time apart from each other, his attractiveness couldn't be denied. His beige mocha skin was flawless. Not a scar or spot in sight. Those hazel eyes glared deeply at her, as if they were staring right into her soul. He wasn't packing in the muscle department, but he didn't need to. Standing at six feet four, Troy stole the attention from any room, and right now, he had her undivided attention.

"Sab."

Unable to help herself, she felt her cheeks grow hot after his voice settled into her ears. He was the only person who gave her that nickname, and every time she heard him call her that, it made her melt inside with pleasure.

"What do you want, Troy?" she asked in a hostile tone. "You've been pestering me with texts, wanting to talk, so talk."

Just because he had rocked up here looking fine as ever and called her by his nickname for her, didn't change the facts. It didn't matter what feelings he had suddenly evoked out of her. Their relationship was long over and dusted. She was only letting him say his little piece, so he could get whatever closure he needed, then she would send him on his merry way.

"Well would you mind letting me in?" he queried, noticing how stand-offish she was acting and standing. Keeping her door halfway open so that he couldn't see the rest of her apartment definitely had him feeling some type of way.

"I don't think that's a good idea," she countered, seeing the disappointment grow in his eyes.

"But I wanna sit down and talk to you, Sab," he explained calmly. "Like grown adults do."

*Sabrina said nothing in return and just stared at him carefully, trying to decide if he was really being genuine or not. **Maybe you should just let him in? Besides, you can stand while he sits and attempts to win you back before letting him know that he's lost you for good.***

"Alright then." She agreed reluctantly before opening up her door wider. "You can come in."

So she let him in, watching closely as he sauntered through her apartment and headed toward her main living area. While he took a seat on her leather sofa, she stayed standing by her kitchen countertop, waiting for him to speak up.

"Sab... I want you back."

Sabrina released a loud scoff, followed by a giggle before full uncontrol-

lable laughter. Troy gave her a hurt look which made her cease her laughter. "Oh, I'm sorry," she announced sarcastically. "Was that not a joke?"

"Am I laughing?"

"No you ain't," she retorted, disliking the attitude she could hear in his voice. "That's why I'm confused, because it must be a joke."

"Sab, what part of I love you do you not get?"

"Nigga, you only love me now that I've moved on. This energy was nowhere to be found when we were in a relationship, when you used to abandon me for days with no calls or texts just so you could be with other bitches!" Her face scrunched up with fury as she watched the guilt sweep across his face.

"I'm a changed man, Sab. I swear," he announced. He may have sounded sincere, but she just wasn't buying it. "Sab... I don't want to live without you. I can't live without you."

"Yes you can," she snapped. "You're breathing right now, ain't you?"

"Yeah, but th—"

"Exactly. So quit acting like you have to be with me because you do—"

"Sab, I almost committed suicide."

His statement instantly made her freeze up. She gave him a petrified, wide-eyed stare, not sure what to say in return to what he had revealed.

"Because I didn't want to spend another day on this earth without you," he announced, getting up from his seat. "I love you, Sabrina. And I'm not going to be able to stop loving you."

Sabrina watched as he walked right up to her, with an assertive gaze plastered on his face. He knew what he wanted, and it was her. That was one thing he wasn't about to back down on.

"And I know," he began, placing his hand on the side of her waist, "that you love me too."

With one hand on her waist, he was able to pull her nearer and lean in toward her lips. Not even trying to stop him, Sabrina let him plant his lips on hers and start the kiss. It was a sweet kiss. A kiss that she didn't even realize she had missed until now.

First it started off as an innocent kiss before turning into a full battle of the tongues, and Sabrina found herself infatuated. He had sparked a fire inside of her that she'd tried to put out for so long but failed to do so successfully.

"Oh my... Oh my God, Troy."

Even as quiet as she tried to remain, it was impossible. Especially with how good he was hitting it from the back. And the fact that they were doing this on her couch? Yeah, Sabrina couldn't believe how good it all felt. After their break, the nigga still knew how to fuck her right. She could still hear her moans despite Troy turning up her TV to mask them. She didn't want her neighbors to hear what was going on at all, so she grabbed the nearest pillow and bit into it.

Masking her moans was the least of her worries because since her eyes were closed, she failed to notice the turning of her doorknob. But she definitely heard the sound of keys dropping to the floor. Her eyes immediately popped open only to see the heartbreak and anguish settled within his eyes. Then he lifted up his shirt and pulled his glock out of his waistband, pointing it straight at her.

"Sabrina, we discussed this though... What the hell happened to you blocking his number, forgetting all about him, and moving on for good?"

"I don't know what came over me." She cried, feeling distraught at remembering memories of Kadeem bursting in on her cheating. "I never meant to hurt him."

"Man... I'm just glad he didn't shoot you, or we would have had a real serious issue on our hands," Monalisa commented with a frown. "So what now?"

Sabrina gave her a blank stare; therefore, Monalisa decided to keep on talking.

"What happens with you and Troy? 'Cause we all know what you had with Kadeem is dead."

The mention of her relationship with Kadeem being dead made her heart sink further, but she knew it was the truth. After what she'd done, she knew he would never want to see her ever again.

"I don't know," she muttered bitterly, wiping her wet cheeks dry.

"Well I guess that's just something you need to figure out on your own," Mona stated simply before deciding to start on her other younger sister who sat quietly in her seat. "Solána?"

"Yeah?"

"You've been awfully quiet," she commented knowingly. "Care to tell us what happened with Kisan?"

Solána sighed deeply at the mention of his name.

"Well... we fucked," she bluntly said before adding, "And then when we were done, he got dressed, and said it was all a mistake."

"Was it?" Monalisa asked curiously.

"A mistake?" Another deep sigh left Solána's lips. "Absolutely not. I wanted him, but I guess he just didn't want me."

"But you said he told you he loved you," Sabrina chimed in, sniffling gently. "Surely that must count for him wanting you despite his decision to end things."

Solána didn't know what to say in response to her sister. Originally, in the back of her mind, Kisan telling her that he loved her had all just been a part of his ploy to slide between her thighs. But the more she thought about it, the more she wasn't sure. All she kept on seeing was the torn look on his face. Why he was so torn, Solána didn't get. He didn't need to be torn, but he seemed to want to make things difficult for himself. He could still be a great father to Luciana and be her man.

But in Kisan's mind, the two couldn't co-exist. The love that he had for Solána was something pure. A love that he hadn't had before. He knew that his love for her wasn't going anywhere, but he still dearly loved his daughter. Luciana being surrounded by a positive family was all he ever wanted. If that made him old-fashioned and traditional, then so be it.

Kisan looked down at his iPad screen, examining the newest Ferrari model that would be delivered to his company tomorrow. His finger played around with it, enabling him to clearly examine the car's exterior and zoom in on its features. Just when he was ready to look at the next car model, his office door opened, and Khaleeq came storming in, the fury radiating off his face.

"I'm going to kill him!" Khaleeq's yell sounded through the entire office and the entire building too. "I'm going to fucking kill him!"

A soft sigh left Kisan's lips, already aware of who Khaleeq was talking about.

"What did he do this time?"

"He went to west Miami and started shooting niggas on sight, Mace. He shot our soldiers for no fuckin' reason!"

CHAPTER 2

"What the fuck is wrong with you? You know how lucky you are that no one's dead? No one's dead, which means I don't need to fuck you up, but believe me, I want to. Why the fuck are you acting like such an idiot?"

Khaleeq's questions didn't faze Kadeem. He could hear the irritation and disgust within his cousin's voice, but it didn't change his nonchalant mood.

"Are you going to answer, or do you want me to make you answer?"

Kisan's threatening question didn't faze him in the slightest either. His entire attitude had changed ever since two days ago; the day that he had felt his entire heart being ripped out. Kadeem had never had a girl cheat on him before. Well if he had, then he'd never seen it until two days ago when he walked in on his girlfriend getting fucked from the back.

I should have known better than to trust a bitch like her foul ass.

Regret was the only thing that filled him. Regret from not killing the nigga that was getting comfortable in his pussy. Even though he had lifted a gun to Sabrina, he knew he would never be able to shoot her, especially with how much he loved her. She was to blame for his outburst at West Miami, shooting up soldiers and not caring if they were dead or alive. He was being reckless, but he didn't care. It was her fault, and at that moment, he just needed to take his anger out on something, or better yet, someone.

His cousins believed that he had gone mad, and Kadeem believed them completely. Because he had gone mad with anguish and shame that the girl he had fallen for had played him like this. He wasn't about to stress too much though, because he knew exactly how to make her pay.

Hours later, Kadeem had been able to leave his cousins after hearing their long tirade of threats and lectures. He now stood by his door and slowly opened it up, only to be greeted to her gorgeous yet remorseful looking face.

Fuck! I hate her beautiful ass.

The only thing he wished to be able to do was hug her dearly and kiss her. But the annoyance within him had run too deeply to enable him to do that. He couldn't even stand to look at her for too long, and she could see it too because he refused to keep firm eye contact with her.

"Kadeem, I'm so sorr—"

"Save it," he cut her off abruptly. "Just come in."

Seeing his text message early this morning, requesting to see her, caught Sabrina off guard. After what she had done, she didn't think he would want to see her ever again. If she was him, she wouldn't want to see her ever again. But he did want to see her, and for that, Sabrina wasn't about to turn him down. She was hoping that he would be willing to give her a chance to explain things, and hopefully, just hopefully, they could move past this.

She walked through his apartment, staring familiarly at the famous paintings on his white walls of his favorite rappers, Snoop Dogg and Jay Z, admiring the layout of his apartment from how his expensive furniture sat in the center of his living area. Just when she thought he would tell her to take a seat, he started heading up the staircase to his bedroom.

"Kadeem, don't you want to talk down here?"

"No." He continued walking up the stairs, refusing to turn to look at her. "Upstairs."

Not wanting to anger him, she followed in pursuit, quickly walking up each step until reaching the doorway of his bedroom.

She entered inside, first spotting his king-sized bed in the center of the room, neatly laid. Memories of them being intimate together and the memories of them cuddling flashed in her mind. Knowing that she messed that up all for Troy, really pissed her off.

"Have a seat."

Sabrina looked at his leather sofa, positioned by the side of his bed, and walked over to it. As confused as she was, she decided to just listen and wait for him to explain what was going on.

"Close your eyes."

She wanted to protest, but her inner voice told her to just remain silent and listen. So that's what she continued to do, shutting her eyes and waiting for him to say what he wanted. There was silence between them for a few minutes, and Sabrina was tempted to open her eyes to see what he was doing, until she felt his hand on her shoulder.

"Do you trust me, Sabrina?"

She nodded before deciding that a nod wasn't enough. "I do, Dee. I'm so sorry about what I did, and I just really want to explai—"

"And you will," he said, interrupting her again. "As soon as I'm done."

"Done with what?"

He didn't respond. Instead, Sabrina felt a piece of fabric cover her lids, and before she knew it, he had blindfolded her.

"Kadeem?"

"Just relax," he ordered.

She obeyed, deciding to just trust him and continue to wait. But trusting him seemed more and more like a struggle when she felt her hands being tied together followed by her legs.

"Kadeem, what are you doi..."

Then he removed her blindfold, giving her the ability to see her surroundings again. She looked down at her hands to see them tied by cable ties and her legs too.

"Kadeem, why have you tied me up?"

The fear in her voice was unmissable. All she kept thinking was that something horrible was going to happen. She didn't want to think about Kadeem killing her, but that was exactly what she believed was going to happen.

"Kadeem," she called out to him, watching him walk toward his en-suite bathroom. He stood in the doorway, and Sabrina watched him motion with his fingers for someone to follow him.

"Valentina, bring your sexy ass in here."

What the hell is going on? She was beyond confused now, but she watched with focused eyes and a bated breath as a woman in red lingerie stepped out of the bathroom.

"Kadeem," Sabrina called his name. "What are you doing?"

However, Kadeem refused to answer her. In fact, at this point, Kadeem refused to even look her way. He just acted like she didn't exist, and his attention remained on his new friend, Valentina. Valentina was a beauty indeed. Dark skinned, thick, and curvy in all the right places, and anxious to please Kadeem.

"Ready to show me what the mouth do, baby?" Kadeem lustfully asked, allowing her to grab his hand.

"Yes, daddy," she responded, grabbing one of his fingers and placing it into her mouth.

Sabrina watched with shocked eyes as Valentina began sucking on his finger, swirling her tongue vigorously around it and looking at him alone, acting as if Sabrina wasn't tied up while sitting on his sofa and watching the pair. Then Kadeem released his finger out of her mouth and started leading her toward his king-sized bed.

Before Sabrina knew it, she was watching the pair of them kiss each other and fondle each other. He stroked her breasts while she stroked his dick in his pants, and the more Sabrina watched, the more she couldn't believe it.

He was never letting me off the hook! He's tied me here so I can watch him have sex with this girl, as his revenge. His sweet revenge.

Sabrina had hit the jackpot indeed because that's exactly what Kadeem had done. He wanted her to feel the same betrayal that he had felt the day he walked in on her having sex on her couch. He wanted her to feel the same hurt and shame that he had felt. And to make things even worse, he wasn't going to give her the same option that he'd had of walking away from the situation. She had to sit there and watch every part of the show.

Tears began to run down Sabrina's face as she watched the two of them passionately tongue each other down, like two lovers that never wanted to be apart from each other. It sucked to see him enjoying something that she believed that only they would do together. But nothing sucked more than when Valentina started giving him head, and his groans filled the room. That wasn't even the worst bit though. The worst bit came when Kadeem tore her lingerie off her body, sucked her nipples, and then made her get on her knees in front of him, allowing him to fuck her from the back.

The same position that Troy had fucked Sabrina in.

Kadeem then looked up from Valentina, staring at Sabrina and seeing the endless tears flowing out of her eyes.

"Happy birthday, Sabrina," he said with a light groan before thrusting back into Valentina.

Sabrina only cried more once realizing that they were supposed to go to the DR today on her birthday. It was his gift to her. But now he had decided to give her a new gift.

Revenge served ice cold.

SOLÁNA WOULD BE a liar if she said that Cleo, the manager of Rose's Fashions hadn't been on her mind. That Instagram post that she had written was something that Solána couldn't forget about. She badly wanted to know what Cleo thought Solána had done to run her out of her store, which is why she now stood outside her new store located in East Miami.

Solána exhaled softly before pushing open the front door and heading inside. Her eyes marveled upon the sights of the store. It was much more upscale and elegantly designed than Rose's Fashions last store. She had more clothing on display and a rich color scheme of purple, lilac, and pink.

"Wow, I'd never thought I'd see the day," Cleo announced as she spotted Solána walking through the store. "The woman who ran me out of town is back to stir up more trouble."

Nervously, Solána continued walking up until she reached the front desk where she was greeted by rude glares from Cleo and her workers. Not one to start unnecessary drama, Solána decided to offer an olive branch.

"I'm not here to start any trouble, Cleo. I just want to talk. There's been a misunderstanding, and I want to sort it out. You think I'm behind you losing your store, but I promise you I'm not."

"Then who the hell is?" Cleo asked defensively with an arched brow.

"I don't know, but if you explain to me what happened, then I can try to get to the bottom of things."

So Cleo led her to the back office and told her all she knew. How a guy in a suit had come to her store and thrown a whole bunch of papers her way, telling her that she needed to close down her store, or she would have lawsuits coming her way. He also threw a bunch of fancy words her way and told her she didn't have a choice. However, not being a gullible person, Cleo decided to ignore him and carry on Rose's Fashions until the next week he came back with more men. Only this time instead of just papers, they brought guns. She had been terrified of losing her life that day, and her son was more important to her than anything. She couldn't die because she had a son to take care of, and if he didn't have her, then he wouldn't have anyone. Cleo willingly signed whatever papers they had and gave up her store, agreeing to leave and never come back. Without even needing to think about it, Solána knew who was behind kicking Cleo out her store. That's why he was so overly interested in knowing the location of her store.

"What the... she said she's going to run you out your store?"

"Basically, yeah," Solána answered. *"I'm trying not to worry about her, but she's got my workers spooked."*

"I see, and a few doors down you said?"

"Yeah. But she's literally just started, so I don't see how she plans to run me out. I've been in the game longer than her and have more connects."

Solána had never been angrier. He had interfered with something that had absolutely nothing to do with him, and for that, she knew she needed to give him a piece of her mind. Fuck whatever was going on between them; he had gotten involved with her business and basically threatened to take the life of a business rival. Solána was surely going to give him a piece of her mind right this instant.

The first place she pulled up to was his penthouse, only to be told by the front receptionist in an overly cheerful voice that "Mr. Williams is not at home at the moment." That cheerful tone of hers only pissed Solána off further, but she still needed to figure out where Kisan was.

There was only one other place she guessed he could be, and that would be at his car rental company. Since today was a Thursday, he would be working. Unless he was working his other unlawful side hustle.

An hour later, she arrived at his company. Despite it being her first time visiting, she didn't seem to be uncomfortable in the new environment. Maybe it was the anger that had given her so much confidence to walk up in the building without a care in the world.

"How can I help you?"

When she got to the front desk, she was greeted to a white attractive male with friendly green eyes.

"Is Kisan Williams in his office?"

"Yes, but he's in the mid... Excuse me, Miss! Where are you going?"

"I'm going to pay him a visit," she simply said, now walking past the front desk and heading through the main building.

"But you can't just go through, Miss! He's the middle of an important mee... Miss!"

Solána refused to turn back or even give a response to the receptionist. She just kept on walking until she reached a black staircase.

Not sure where she was going but determined to keep pressing on, Solána headed up onto the second floor, praying that Kisan's office would appear to her sooner than later.

Solána was highly impressed with the architecture of Kisan's company. It was not only a grand building, but it had a state of the art design with expensive looking polished concrete floors, various luxury car portraits hanging on light gray walls, and seating areas with furniture that looked like they cost a fortune.

As she walked through a corridor that led to three main doors, Solána sighed with relief to see Kisan's name in an elegant silver font on one of the mahogany doors. Without even hesitating, she immediately stormed toward it and barged in, ready to attack, only to quickly look mortified when she saw a bunch of people in suits. They were seated around a mahogany desk in the far-left corner of the spacious room.

Kisan who was at the head of the table, looked perplexed by Solána's arrival. She had never showed up at his company, and now that she had, he didn't know what to think. The last time they had seen each other had been at her apartment, and things hadn't ended well.

"Solána?" His tone was a mixture of both confusion and worry, and he got up from his seat to walk toward her. "What are you doing here?"

Her heart warmed a little at the worry she could hear in his voice. But that still didn't change her mood, especially with what she knew of him threatening Cleo. She didn't care about his colleagues being present because as far as she was concerned, they already knew what type of man he was, and they probably had something to do with the situation too.

"You interfere with my personal life, and now I found out that you've interfered with my business life too? Threatening a business riv—"

"Have you lost your damn mind?" His eyes widened with complete seriousness as he kept a short distance between them.

Sensing the complete shift in his attitude toward her made her heart race with apprehension. Storming into his office while he was in the middle of a meeting, just didn't seem that much of a good idea anymore.

"You threatened Cle—"

He instantly cut her off, this time his voice was much lower than before so that only the two of them could hear him. "Nah, clearly you have lost your mind, comin' up in here like you fuckin' own the place, but I promise you I'm 'bout to remind you who owns this shit." His tone was tense, jaw twitching and fists clenched by his sides. He was angry, there was no doubt about it, but Solána couldn't change how she felt.

Kisan then turned around to face the seated women and men. "Could everyone please excuse me for a minute? I just need to quickly handle something."

He walked to the right, quickly pulling along the sliding room dividers before separating the rooms completely.

"Take a seat," Kisan sternly ordered, his back still facing her as he locked the dividers.

"I'd rather stand."

"And I'd rather fuck you up right now, but clearly you're pissed off about something, and I want to get to the bottom of it. Sit down, Solána."

Solána eyed his work desk and decided to obey. She walked over to it before taking her seat on his black leather chair. By now, he had turned away from the dividers and was now making his way toward her.

"What's the problem?"

"You threatened Cleo and made her leave her store."

"She was giving you problems, so I sorted her out."

"I never asked you to do that shit!"

"And who the fuck you yelling at?"

"You, nigga! You were the one that broke up with me, so why are you still interfering with my life?"

"The situation with Cleo happened before I ended things. She still was a problem, so like I just fuckin' said, in case your dumb ass didn't hear me the first time, I sorted her out."

Soláha immediately crossed her arms, sighing and huffing with defeat at his words. It seemed like no matter what she said, Kisan wasn't about to budge. He was right, and she was wrong. That's what he believed, so that's what everyone needed to believe apparently. She couldn't stand his arrogant ass.

"And you can get sorted out too if you keep fuckin' trying a nigga."

"Fuck you, Kisan," she concluded, pushing her seat back and adamant on leaving. He clearly wasn't going to see things her way, so what was the point of her staying? However, just as she stood up and turned to walk away from his desk, Kisan had already walked around his desk and came to stand behind her.

"Where the hell you goin'?" he asked, grabbing her arm and keeping her put. His touch instantly made her insides fire up, but she chose to ignore it.

"Away from you," she retorted, turning to face him and trying to push him away, only to fail when he grabbed her hand in his. "Kisan, let me go."

"I can't," he admitted truthfully, shocking her. The truth was seeing her here had only made his feelings for her showcase once more, making him realize how much he had missed her, and it didn't help at how good she looked. Dressed in a tight-fitting summer dress that shaped her body well only made him admire her. The color lilac never looked better on her.

"You ended us, remember?" she smugly reminded him with an arched brow. "Therefore, letting me go is the only option that you have."

She was right. He had ended things between them. But seeing her now was only reminding him of the one thing he couldn't deny: he had made a mistake.

"Sol..."

"What?" she queried, staring deeply into his eyes, seeing the conflict he was having with his internal thoughts. "What could you possibly have to say no—"

Her words were instantly cut short by his lips. His lips that had landed onto hers and were desperate to give her some attention. He wasn't sure how she would take his sudden kiss, but by her going along with his direction and not pulling their lips apart, he knew that she'd wanted him just as bad as he'd wanted her.

And that was the honest truth. Solána did want him. Her being angry with what he had done didn't change that. She would always want him. How could she not? He always did look sexy in a suit, and now that she was in his presence while he wore one, Solána wanted every last part of him.

She broke their kiss, reached for his belt, and quickly started unbuckling it, making Kisan look down with surprise but also excitement at her actions. They were really about to do this, with all his co-workers next door. But neither of them gave a damn.

Solána found herself unable to carry on getting his pants off when he reached for her hand. She looked up into his honey brown eyes to see the lust cradled within them.

"Come here," he said, reaching for her hand and taking her over to his window wall behind his desk that overlooked the main entrance and front reception. She sensed his plan without him even needing to speak up, but Solána wasn't sure about it.

"Won't everyone see?"

"Nah," he voiced coolly, gently pushing her up against the glass and pulling up her dress. "It's a one-way window wall. Only I can see through it. So no one's about to see me murdering that pussy but me."

Solána blushed at his remark, her heart beating faster and faster with each passing moment. Then her hands went straight back on his pants, anxiously unzipping them and pulling them down. As instantaneous as this was, she wanted it to happen more than ever. Not being intimate with Kisan was something that she missed, and now that the opportunity had arose, she wasn't about to pass it up.

"Sol…"

"Yeah?" She was too focused with pulling his boxers down and bringing out his manhood, rather than listening, which is why Kisan grabbed her chin and lifted it up so she was forced to look at him.

"I still stand by what I said," he explained wholeheartedly. "But I love you." She sighed deeply, not uttering a word in response. "I'm sorry that I keep on fuckin' up. Honestly, a nigga is just so damn torn these days. But what happened with that girl and her store, I did that shit because I wanted to. Ain't no one ever gon' be able to disrespect the girl I love and get away it. No mothafuckin' one. And that's just something you're going to get used to, Sol."

Solána felt herself zone out when she heard him mention her getting used to things. If she was going to get used to him doing things his way, then wouldn't that mean that they would be together? Wouldn't that mean that she would be his girl and their breakup would be no more?

Not wanting to ruin the moment, Solána decided to save her questions for another time. Right now, she just wanted him inside of her and fucking her. So she did exactly what she wanted. Allowed him to fuck her. Fuck her into forgetting about all the anger she felt toward him when coming here; fuck her into forgetting about all the pain he had caused her over the past few weeks; and fuck her into remembering how undeniably in love she was with him.

Her soft moans and whimpers sounded as he quickly thrusted his thickness into her. Deeper and deeper, he pushed fully inside her, his long fingers digging into her ass cheeks, wanting her to feel every last ridge on his shaft. His heavy breathing and groans could be heard, trying to keep himself at a steady volume because his co-workers were still on the other side of his office, waiting for his return.

Solána wanted to cry, scream, and shout all at the same damn time because of how good it all hurt. They weren't using protection, and things were very intense. His shaft was twitching and pulsating against her tight walls, truly driving her crazy; crazy with love and lust for him. She never wanted to lose this pleasure. It was an aphrodisiac that she never wanted to come down off.

Kisan buried his face in her neck and breathed heavily against her skin and used more force to pound his dick into her pussy. Her pussy that he could feel dripping all along the exterior of his dick, and with each pound, wet squishy sounds could be heard. And it turned him on even more to know that he had gotten her this hyped up.

Solána could feel herself getting dizzy. Dizzy at how bad the pleasure was. All she could feel was Kisan fucking her, faster and harder. She was enjoying every single part of it. He kept his biceps wrapped around her waist as he gave her what she wanted. What he knew she desperately needed.

His wet kisses on her throat and neck only drove her crazier. She felt nasty. The kind of nasty that made you feel good knowing you were doing something bad. And they were doing something bad. Having sex against his office wall with people anxiously waiting on the other side for Kisan's arrival. But fuck them. They didn't matter.

Solána's moans heighted as Kisan continued to thrust deeper and harder. Her nails were digging into his back, through his shirt, and she had to secure her thighs around his torso tighter to keep from having his dick slip out her wetness.

"Fuck! I love you, peanut," he groaned deeply against her neck, feeling tears fill his eyes. "I love you, I love this pussy, I love you how you make a nigga feel... I ain't ever gonna stop lovin' you, baby. This my shit foreva."

Solána suddenly felt a wetness hit her neck, and she looked down to see tears flowing out of Kisan's eyes. Seeing him cry while they had sex was a strange feeling to her. A part of her was saddened by his tears, but another part of her absolutely loved it. Their intense love making had brought tears to his eyes.

"I lo... I love yo... you too," she whispered breathlessly, lifting his chin and locking lips with him.

CHAPTER 3

H appy birthday, sis. I love you.

Monalisa sent a quick text to Sabrina, knowing that she didn't want to celebrate her birthday at all, especially because of what she had done to Kadeem. Mona just hoped she was okay and having quality time to herself. She looked up at the oak door in front of her, in disbelief that she was back here. As she stared at the front door, her mind seemed to race with conflicted thoughts. She had placed herself in a very uncomfortable position, and she had no escape route. She was stuck.

Knock! Knock!

Her nerves overfilled her as she anxiously waited for the door to open, praying that it would be April and not anyone else to open the door. She wasn't sure how she would react upon seeing him. However, she was faced with the very choice that she didn't want.

The door slowly opened, and his sexy face appeared. That face that she hadn't been able to get out of her head. The face that she dreamt about most nights, and the face that she pictured while masturbating.

She didn't say a word. Instead, she found herself staring deeply into his brown eyes and hoping he would just let her in without saying a word. His eyes drifted up and down her body before finally landing back on her eyes.

"You good?"

It took Monalisa a minute, but she plucked up the courage to give him a simple head nod before deciding to woman up and stop acting weak.

"I'm good," she casually responded. "You?"

"Just fine," he answered before opening up the door wider for her to step inside. "April's 'round the back."

"Got it. Thanks." She made a step forward inside his home only for him to step forward at the same time, trying to get outside, bumping right into her.

"My bad," he mumbled, looking closely at her.

"No worries." She quickly stepped away, not wanting to get too close to him. But with how close she had gotten with him already, there wasn't anything beyond that.

"Mona!"

Hearing April's call for her instantly made her sigh a breath of relief. Instead of paying any more attention to Khaleeq, she sauntered through their home and left him standing by the door, sensing his eyes glued onto her figure as she walked away.

When she met April in the garden, sitting on a picnic mat, the front door slammed shut, and another breath of relief left Mona's lips.

Khaleeq Williams was a one-time mistake, and she was certain that what had happened between them was not going to happen again. They'd had too much to drink that night and gotten carried away. One thing that Monalisa knew for sure was that she wasn't getting drunk around him ever again.

After finalizing wedding details with April, Monalisa decided to run a few errands before heading home. These days, thinking about her sisters was her main priority because they were truly going through it. Much worse than her. And as the oldest, it was Monalisa's duty to look after and protect them. She had to be strong for them, no matter what. So her little personal issues with the fiancé of her latest client would have to be swept under the rug and forgotten about.

Getting home was bittersweet. Bitter because she had forgotten to visit one store while running errands, but sweet because she could lay on her comfy couch and binge watch her favorite Netflix series, *Dear White People.*

She greatly emphasized with one of the main characters, Sam. Because while having to deal with the racist problems and pressures of being a black student in a predominantly white university, she also had to deal with her own personal conflicts. It was difficult and discouraging, but nonetheless, Sam had to deal with them both.

Monalisa couldn't imagine dealing with her own problems and her sisters problems at the same time. There was only one she chose to deal with, and it was her sisters. They would always come first.

Ooh, now I'll never get over you until I find something new
That get me high like you do
Listen my to heart go ba-dum, bo—

"Hey, Auntie."

Seeing her aunt's name appear on the caller ID, warmed her heart up. She was always glad to hear from her, even though they talked like every week.

"Mona, love," she greeted her with that caring and tender tone of hers that Mona loved.

They talked for what felt like hours. Monalisa caught her up on her week so far and how work was. She was even tempted to tell her what she had done with her client's fiancé. The fact that Mona hadn't told her sisters meant that she had an itchy conscience; an itchy conscience that was just dying to let out the truth and tell someone. Just when Mona had plucked up the courage to reveal all, her doorbell sounded.

"Auntie, someone's at my door," she explained. "Can I call you back?"

"Sure thing," her aunt responded in an understanding tone.

Monalisa ended the call and slowly got up from her seat. As reluctant as she was to open the door, interest had captivated her to know who was on the other side. But upon opening the door, interest no longer captivated her. Bewilderment did instead.

"What are you doing here?"

He still looked sexy from when she had seen him early this afternoon. Dressed in a black Nike tracksuit from head to toe, with matching Nike Air Jordan Retro 12's on his feet, Khaleeq looked like a dark knight that had come to put her out of her misery; her misery of tossing and turning each night with only him in mind; her misery of wanting his lips between her thighs despite knowing that those lips did not belong to her.

"I came to see you," he bluntly replied, keeping a fixed gaze on her which started to make her slightly nervous. Because it reminded her of the fixed gaze he'd had when they had first...

"Why?"

Khaleeq had no response for her query because the truth was, he didn't even truly know why he had come. Okay, maybe he did. Seeing her earlier at his crib definitely had him feeling some type of way. She still looked as gorgeous as ever, and he still found the feelings that he thought were nothing but lust make an appearance at the sight of her.

"To be honest with you," he began, finessing his fingers through his light beard. "A nigga don't even know."

"You don't know why you've come here?"

He shook his head, and his eyes started to do the thing they'd been craving to do since laying eyes on her again: they wandered down her body, admiring everything about what they were seeing. She had changed into casual clothing, leggings and a tank top, but that didn't stop Khaleeq's eyes from loving what they could see.

"Did April forget to tell me something?"

Her mention of April should have triggered him and made him remember about his soon to be wife, but it didn't. It only made him continue to stare silently at her. Again, he shook his head 'no', and Mona found herself still nervous under his gaze.

But her nerves didn't change the fact that she could feel the tension. Without him even being inside her home yet, the tension was strongly brewing with each passing second. And it slightly annoyed

Monalisa. Annoyed her because of how handsome he looked dressed in his black tracksuit. Annoyed at how bad she wanted to run into his arms and kiss him.

"Maybe you should go, Khaleeq," she announced, dropping her eyes to the floor so she would no longer have to stare at him.

"That's what you want?"

Of course not. You know how bad you want him, Mona.

"Look me in the eyes and tell me that's what you want," he suddenly demanded. His demand made the hairs on the back of her neck stand up. Instead of doing as he asked, Monalisa stood in her place and exhaled deeply.

"Mo."

Her name coming out from his lips was a sound she truly wouldn't mind hearing numerous times. His deep voice was captivating, able to reel her in and make her want him worse than before. She felt her chin being lifted up, and her eyes locked onto his.

"Answer me."

His touch felt like electricity on her skin. She froze in her place, feeling paralyzed by his simple yet significant action.

"What do you want?"

"You," she obediently answered in a soft whisper. "I want you."

When his lips landed on her lips, Mona knew that just like their first encounter, he had won her once more. And when he gently pushed her into her home while keeping their lips locked, Mona knew that what they were about to do meant that there was no going back.

Khaleeq was a big fat liar. He knew exactly why he had come here; he just didn't want to admit it. But he didn't have to, because seeing the smile in his eyes as he watched her told her everything she needed to know. He wanted her, and he didn't want to stop having her.

"Khaleeq... you don't have to d—"

"I want to," he explained, pulling her panties down her thighs until they'd reached her ankles and he was able to throw them to the floor. "You've been on my mind since the day I left you. A nigga wants to taste you... every last part of you."

"But... what happened to us never doing this again?"

Khaleeq was silent for a few seconds, staring at her intensely before saying, "Ignore what I said. I want you."

Five minutes was all it took for him to begin his intoxicating dance of driving her wild with his tongue. Monalisa gently moaned as his tongue slowly licked up and down her slit. He began slowly at first, teasing her folds with his wet flesh before increasing his speed and switching things up completely.

A shiver went down her spine as Khaleeq's tongue snaked its way deeper into her wet folds, causing her back to arch up on her bed. Her whimpers and moans became louder as he started to devour her pussy. As his eager tongue dived further, she felt her thighs slowly begin to shake on his shoulders, and her heart ferociously pounded in her chest, making no attempts at slowing down.

Her fingers found their way to the back of his head of waves, pushing him deeper between her legs as he gave her the drug she'd required for the past few days. He was the drug, but his tongue was officially her newest addiction. The addiction that provided her with the most satisfaction and pleasure.

In and out, his tongue darted through her pussy, sending her mind into a whole different world. Ecstasy clouded her brain as his fingers pushed into her while he licked away at her pearl nonstop. What made it even worse was those chestnut eyes of his that refused to break away. Those heavenly eyes would be the death of her. They loved to watch her while she made her love faces and relished in the pleasure that he gave her. She noticed how glossy his thick lips were from her juices, coating not only his lips but his beard too.

Her thighs trembled quicker as his talented tongue continued to lap away, and the pressure between her thighs heightened. His fingers were still pushing and pulling in and out of her, speeding up with each passing heated moment.

Minutes later, Monalisa loudly whimpered, feeling the pressure between her legs reaching overload. Her head fell back, and her eyes closed as her pussy spasmed and tightened around his fingers and tongue. She felt her whole entire body shake as the euphoria came over her like a wave.

Khaleeq willingly drank up every drop of her climax before pressing his nose against her clit, inhaling her deeply. Once seeing that she had recovered from her high, he kissed the top of her pussy softly. Then the next words he spoke made Mona realize that what they were doing was far from over.

"You taste fuckin' amazing, Mo. A nigga could definitely get used to this shit."

They were going to embark on a dangerous affair that neither one of them could get enough of.

WHAT KADEEM HAD DONE to Sabrina had left her traumatized. It had been his own nasty little way of getting back at her for cheating on him, and he had succeeded. He had succeeded in making her feel like shit.

I knew he was crazy, but tying me up and making me watch him fuck another girl? Yeah, he's even crazier than I thought. On my fucking birthday too!

At this moment, Sabrina knew that whatever small hope she'd originally had about them getting back together was completely out the window. They would never be able to rekindle what they'd built together.

Ding!

Sabrina looked down at her phone to see a new text message notification.

Can I see you?

Troy.

As much as Kadeem had hurt her, strangely enough, her feelings for him hadn't gone anywhere. How could they? She had deeply grown fond of him and even started to love him. But cheating on him had been the nail to the coffin, and now that he'd gotten his revenge, she was positive that he would want nothing to do with her.

Sabrina: *Yes.*

Within seconds, his reply came in. *Now?*

Sabrina: *Okay.*

Troy: *I'm on my way, beautiful.*

Getting back with Troy seemed like her only option. The truth was, she didn't want to be alone, especially at a time like this when all she could think about was Kadeem. Troy would have to fill the void that haunted her soul.

CHAPTER 4

*M*an... *how the hell am I going to get her out of my head?* Every night this week, Solána had been the center of his focus. He didn't know how he was supposed to get her out of his head, especially with how strong his feelings were growing for her. And with how good they had gotten it in, in his office last week, she was all he could think about. It had angered him at how she had boldly burst into his meeting, but it turned him on to see her confidence. That confidence that he loved about her.

"Dwaddy, you okay?"

Kisan looked down to his heart in the physical staring up at him with a grin.

"I am now that my favorite person in the whole wide world is with me," he announced, lifting her up so that she could sit on his lap. "How was school, mama?"

"Good," she responded happily, resting her head against his hard chest. "How was work, Dwaddy?"

Luciana was not your average four-year-old. She was extremely intelligent, and yes, she mispronounced a few words from time to time, but having a conversation with her felt like heaven on earth to Kisan.

"Boring," he admitted. "So what did you learn in school today?"

They talked for what felt like hours. He cherished moments like these with his daughter, when he could just listen to her talk, see that excitement light up on her precious little face, and respond to her just as eagerly as she had mustered up conversation.

"Well it's really good to hear that you had a good day at school, mama. You know all daddy wants is for you to be happy."

She nodded with understanding before stating, "And I just want you happy too, Dad."

Hearing her say that brought a permanent smile on his face, and he lovingly looked at her.

"You being happy is my ultimate happiness, mama," he explained. "Always."

"But what makes you happy is imwportant too," she said, mispronouncing the word important, which only made him smile harder. "I don't want you sad."

"But, Lu, remember when you told me that me leaving you and your mom makes you sad? I can't allow that."

Luciana stayed quiet for a while, her focused facial expression showing that she was deep in thought. Then she decided to speak up. "Mom said I should tell you not to go."

Thinking that maybe he had misheard her, his eyes widened, and he reached for her hand, holding it within his before asking her to repeat herself.

"Mom said I should tell you not to leave us."

Kisan sighed deeply as he stared off at the living room walls. *I should have known she put her up to this. What she said isn't something she's ever said before. I see her every day, and she's never once been unhappy about me not living with her and Dazhanae. Wow. I'm really gonna fuck her ass up. She's lucky she's not at home right now.*

Dazhanae was in fact not lucky that she wasn't at home with her daughter and Kisan right now. She was placed in the awkward position of having an impromptu sit down that April had decided to have with her at Nobu, an upscale Japanese-Peruvian restaurant.

"So what is it you needed to talk to me about, girl?" Dazhanae curiously questioned her, watching her take a small sip of her mojito, praying that this sit down would be swift and smooth. She wasn't planning to order any food, only hear what April had to say and then leave.

"I've been thinking a lot about that night... you know, the night we both got drunk."

April had been indeed thinking about that drunken night between them. It had been her main distraction from her wedding which was weeks away. Hearing Dazhanae unintentionally reveal drunk tales about her daughter, Kisan, and his best friend, Lucas, left her conflicted. She had a vast amount of loyalty to Kisan because that was her man's cousin. Extremely close cousin. Feeling like she had this terrible, grave secret was an uneasy feeling that April needed to get rid of. She didn't want to cause a fire, but she could try her very hardest to put it out before it could start.

"I need you to take a DNA test proving that Kisan is the father of Luciana."

Dazhanae thought that she was having a nightmare. Because surely this had to be one very horrific nightmare that she needed to wake up from right this instant.

"Excuse me?" She gave April a look of disgust. "April, I told you that I said a lot of bullshit that night."

"Then prove it to me," she explained coolly. "Take a DNA test proving that he is the father. He doesn't even need to find out; just take a piece of his DNA when he's asleep or something and get Luciana's DNA too."

"Girl, this is fucking crazy, and I don't need to prove anything to you," Dazhanae snapped, secretly feeling terrified deep inside.

"And that's fine," April responded with a simple shrug. "I'll just tell Khaleeq to tell Kisan to get a DNA test himself."

Dazhanae looked at her with an open mouth, realizing what this had now become: a blackmailing situation.

"You wouldn't."

"I would," April confirmed with a firm look. "Look, you may have said bullshit, but I'm just trying to protect my fiancé's cousin. At the end of the day, my loyalty is with Khaleeq's family. I was introduced to you through Kisan. The least I owe to him is to ensure that his daughter is actually his daughter."

Dazhanae wanted to be swallowed up whole by the ground. That was the only thing she was sure would save her from the predicament she was in; the worst predicament she had been in all year. Her own friend was blackmailing her to prove that Kisan was the father of Luciana. Her own precious friend.

A normal mother wouldn't have sweated about the situation. They would have just gotten the test done, proved the paternity, and moved on. But Dazhanae wasn't a normal mother. She was a wicked mother for robbing her daughter the truth of knowing who her real father was. Because he wasn't Kisan.

"I WANT MY BED," Sabrina voiced with a deep sigh. These days, her thoughts consisted of one man and one man alone. And he wasn't the person who she had decided to get back into a relationship with.

"You and me both," Solána responded truthfully before picking up her glass and chugging her vodka down her throat.

"We're not going anywhere," Monalisa announced sternly, frowning at the both of them. "Because you're both going to enjoy this night out that I set up. You've both been going through some shit, so think of this being a way to forget all about your troubles."

"I think my bed is a better way of me forgetting all my troubles," Sabrina said.

"No, Rina," Monalisa disagreed before pushing her cocktail glass toward her. "Drink up and lighten up. You're not going anywhere."

Sabrina sighed and did as she asked, lifting the glass to her lips and drinking from it.

Monalisa had brought her sisters along to an open mic night to cheer them both up. It was due to start in five minutes, and Monalisa prayed that the entertainment would be the right remedy for her sisters' somber moods.

Ding!

You home?

Seeing his message appear on her screen made her blush and fill with lust for him.

No, she quickly typed back. *Out with my sisters.*

Monalisa locked her phone and focused on the empty stage ahead, only to suddenly feel her phone vibrate on her lap, and she picked up her phone to read his text.

I was about to come over and eat you like a pink Starburst but you out with your sisters. Have fun tho.

Monalisa found herself blushing harder at his message and having to squeeze her thighs together in the hopes that it would relieve the fire growing below.

Monalisa: *You tease.*

Monalisa: *You could always come later when I'm back home.*

Khaleeq: *How long will you be?*

Monalisa: *Just a few hours.*

Khaleeq: *A'ight. Hit me up when you're heading home.*

Monalisa: *Okay.*

"Hello, everyone, and thank you for coming to Zizzi's open mic night. First up…"

Monalisa locked her iPhone once more and focused her attention on the stage ahead. She took a quick glance at her sisters to see that they were focused on the stage already.

The first act coming up was a comedian, and when he stepped out, the Winters Sisters were surprised because not only was he white, but he was also very handsome. The surprise came from the fact that they were in a black populated bar. There were hardly any whites in the audience or working in the bar.

"Hello, everyone," his British accent sounded, enticing Solána even more. "I'm Blake. And yes, I'm British, and before you ask, no I'm not related to the royal family in any shape or form. I hate those stuck up motherfuckers."

Everyone immediately let out laughter after he spoke, and Solána found herself completely drawn to him. She wasn't usually enticed by white men, but Blake was a different story. He was pretty tall, fairly muscular, and had olive skin. His eyes were dark brown and hooked you in from their very first glance. He had a light beard that covered his jawline and connected to the mustache around his small, pink lips. On his head sat a full head of hair that had a fresh fade. White boy was fine indeed, and to top it all off, he was actually funny. She laughed at all of his jokes without even feeling like she was forcing herself to laugh.

When his set was over, Solána felt saddened that he was going, but nonetheless glad that he had made her laugh. An hour and a half later, the open mic event was over, and the girls headed back to the bar to grab last minute drinks.

"So how do you guys feel?"

"A lot better," Sabrina answered Monalisa with a wide smile. "This actually helped a lot and was fun. Thank you, sis."

"Yeah, I agree," Solána happily chimed in with a head nod. "Definitely fun. Thanks, sis."

"No worries. It's my job," Monalisa answered before typing away on her phone. "You guys ready to go?" she asked without looking up from her device.

Monalisa: *Heading home.*

Khaleeq: *On my way.*

"Yeah," Sabrina said simply.

"Yup," Solána concluded as she lifted the remaining of her Hennessy and took it to the head.

"Great, then let's g—"

"Excuse me?"

That British accent that had been in her ears over an hour ago had made a comeback. Solána slowly turned around from the bar to see the attractive face of Mr. White Boy.

"Can we help you?" Monalisa asked, staring at him closely.

His eyes were glued on Solána's, but Monalisa had still gone into protective sister mode as she always did.

"Well yes and no... I'd love to get a minute of her time."

Sabrina and Monalisa turned to look at their sister who had remained silent.

"My time?" she finally spoke up.

"Yes," he replied with a smile, revealing his pearly whites. "I couldn't take my eyes off you during my entire set, and I just knew that if I didn't approach you before I left, I would never forgive myself."

"And why's that?"

"Because letting a beauty such as yourself leave my sight would be crime that I would forever punish myself for it."

Charming indeed. That's the first thought that came to Solána's mind. The second thought that came was, *you have a man already.* But that wasn't true anymore. After their heated session at his office, he hadn't hit her up. Not one text or call. And it reminded Solána that their breakup had never ended. She didn't have a man anymore which meant that she was single and free to mingle with whoever she liked.

CHAPTER 5

~ 1 WEEK LATER ~

"Yes, Auntie… I'll come over tomorrow, if that's okay?… Uh-huh, yeah. I'll let them know… What am I doing?" Monalisa's eyes trailed off to look ahead at the shirtless man standing by her window and watching her with a sexy smirk plastered on his lips. "Oh nothing, just chilling… yeah, working from home today."

Khaleeq made his way toward the edge of her bed before climbing on top and gently pulling on her long legs, sliding her down the mattress so that he could have her closer to him.

"Uhh… No, I'm gonna ask her though. Probably yes." Monalisa smiled as he started kissing on her jawline, neck, and throat. "Yeah, sure. I'll bring that myself." When she felt his tongue lick her skin, she found herself unable to contain a giggle because of her ticklish nature. Her giggle was immediately heard by her aunt who wanted to know what was funny. "Nothing, Auntie. I just remembered a funny joke… Yeah, sure." Khaleeq continued to kiss on her skin, watching her carefully and anxiously waiting for her to come off the phone. "Alrightie, I'll see you tomorrow then. Bye. I love you too."

Once she had ended the call, Khaleeq was on her like a bee to honey. He grabbed her phone, throwing it to the side, and grabbed her neck before sealing their lips together with a kiss.

"Mmh... Leeq."

For the past fourteen nights, Khaleeq had spent more than half of those nights with Monalisa. Ten nights exactly, and they had been the best, most exhilarating nights of Monalisa's life. He hadn't even known her long, but somehow, he knew her body really well. He knew how to reach all her pleasure spots, and it was addicting to say the least.

She couldn't get enough of him at this point. He was her crack, her quick fix, her everything. Having him around brought her constant joy; being able to text him whenever they were apart truly enticed Monalisa. Her enticement helped disguised the guilt she felt knowing that he was getting married in a few weeks, and they were fooling around as if he wasn't tied down to someone else. It helped disguise the uneasy feeling she felt about April ever finding out what they were doing.

At this point, she didn't want April to find out. Being with Khaleeq brought feelings out of her that she hadn't felt in so long. Feelings that she wasn't willing to sacrifice despite knowing that she would always be nothing than the other woman.

"You hungry?"

Sabrina shook her head 'no' at Troy's question, keeping her arms hugged around her legs. Today was her day off from working at Solána Rose, and she had decided to spend the day with Troy.

"You wanna watch a movie?"

Again, she shook her head 'no' and rested her chin against her knees.

"Sabrina..." She observed as he moved toward the couch and sat on the empty seat next to her. "What do you wanna do?"

Getting back with Troy was a decision that she had willingly made. Did she still have some regret about him? One hundred percent. But could she change what she had done? Absolutely not. The only thing she could do now was deal with the consequences of her actions.

"Let's watch a movie," Sabrina announced, giving him a weak smile.

He gave her a surprised look because of her sudden change of attitude. "You sure?"

"Yeah," she agreed with sure head nods. "Watching a movie is cool."

"What do you want to watch?"

"Anything on Netflix will do," she said. "You choose."

"Alright, babe."

While Troy explored Netflix and tried to find a movie or series for them to watch, Sabrina stared at the plasma screen, feeling hopeless and disheartened. She didn't know if these feelings would ever go away, but she hoped to God that they did. Because living like this was not something she was sure she could do for the next few months. It would only get worse. She missed Kadeem too much.

Ding!

Sabrina slowly reached into her front pocket for her phone, assuming that one of her sisters or closest friends had messaged her, but they hadn't.

Leave and come outside.

It was a message from Kadeem. And yes, she hadn't deleted his number. But right now, she was confused by his text.

Sabrina: *Sorry?*

His reply was instant: *Leave that clown's crib and come downstairs. Now.*

Sabrina: *Where are you?*

Kadeem: *Where do you think?*

She took a quick glance at Troy to see him preoccupied with choosing what they should watch. As curious as she was to go and meet Kadeem outside, she knew she couldn't just go. What was she supposed to say?

Sabrina: *I can't just leave, Kadeem. What am I supposed to say?*

Kadeem: *That's your own personal problem.*

Kadeem: *You either come out now or I come and get you. Your choice.*

Sabrina swallowed hard after his response, biting her lip nervously as she contemplated on how to get herself out of Troy's home.

"Troy... I need to quickly call my aunt," she spoke up, exhaling lightly and lifting her feet off the couch.

"Oh, okay. I'll wait."

"No, you can start it without me," she said, placing her feet into her pink Fenty slides. "She's been expecting my call because she needs to tell me something really important. Family issue apparently."

It was the quickest, convincible lie that Sabrina could come up with, and to her surprise, it actually worked. Because before she knew it, she was outside Troy's apartment building and scanning her surroundings for Kadeem. When she spotted his Maybach limo parked on a side street, she immediately walked over to it. Once close to it, the passenger door opened, and she made a beeline inside. She climbed in and pulled the door shut behind her.

Laying eyes on him sitting comfortably on the back seat made her heart skip a beat. She took a seat opposite him and exhaled deeply. The last time she had seen him had been that day he had invited her to his penthouse and made her watch him have...

"I hope you're not about to do a repeat of the last time I saw you, making me watch you fuck some other bitch," she retorted, folding her arms against her chest with dismay.

"Consider that a lesson for cheating on me with that fool that I still have a pending bullet for."

"Don't, Kadeem," she pleaded, not wanting Kadeem to hurt Troy. "None of it was his fault."

"You cheated on me with him," he snapped with a mean mug. "How is that not your fault and his? He knew you were in a relationship."

"He didn't," Sabrina admitted. "He didn't know that I was in a relationship with you at all."

"Oh, is that right?" He smirked at her. "So you let this nigga believe that you were single this whole time? So the bullet I have for him really should be for your dumbass?"

Sabrina said nothing and looked at him with a guilty look. He was still so pissed with her. She could see it in his eyes, hear it in his voice, and she also knew that he had every right to be. Cheating on him had been wrong.

"Kadeem, look... I know I hurt you, and I sincerely apologize for that. What I did was really fucked up, and if I could take it back, I swear I would. If I could make things right, I swear I would," she announced sincerely, but from the stern look on Kadeem's face, she could tell he hadn't bought her apology.

"You think getting back with that nigga is making things right?" he rudely asked her. "Getting back with the very same nigga you cheated on me with?"

"I didn't know what else to do," she explained truthfully. "I missed you, and I needed someone to fill the void. So I got back with him."

"Do you love him?"

"No," she promised. "Not at all."

"But you still have feelings for him! Letting him dick you down and shit!"

"Not as much as I have feelings for you, Kadeem!"

"So why the fuck did you fuck him!" he yelled back at her, sitting up in his seat.

"Because I felt sorry for him," she cried, feeling her tears now sliding down her cheeks. "He said he couldn't live without me. He tried to commit suicide, Dee."

"So you basically let this nigga guilt trip you with suicide," he retorted. "You're dumber than I thought."

"I'm dumber than you thought? Kadeem, he tried to take his own life."

"And you don't have any fuckin' evidence to prove that shit for sure; you're just going by what he told you."

"So what am I supposed to do? Just act like I didn't hear him say he tried to take his own life because of me? Then let him wound up dead one day in his apartment?" she asked with a frown.

"You should have never let him have what belonged to me. End of."

Sabrina didn't even know what to say in response. She didn't know what to say anymore, because nothing was going to change the past. What had been done had been done.

"Again, I'm so sorry, Kadeem," she apologized once again. "I know you hate me, and I know there's nothing I can do to change that."

"You're right; there isn't anything you can do to change that," he fumed. "Get the fuck out my car, Sabrina."

All she could do was stare into his eyes and see the complete hatred he had for her. She decided to obey, opening his car door and leaving, feeling completely heartbroken by this whole situation.

Trying to convince himself that he still didn't love her was impossible. The love he had for her, despite what she had done to hurt him, still existed. He had tried so hard the past couple of days to get her out of his system, but sadly, he had failed. Having sex with other women didn't help get Sabrina Winters out his head. He would just have to try harder.

Thirty minutes later, Kadeem had pulled to the location of an important meeting that he had set up. Walking into the warehouse, he felt confident but nonetheless cautious. This meeting was with some very important men to him, but he couldn't be naïve and not have himself alert.

Once entering the main room, he noticed how the eyes of three main Serbian men were on him; the men that were going to help him take what he required.

"You're late," the one in the middle announced in a stern tone, staring at him stoically.

"I ain't late," he cockily answered, moving deeper into the room until he reached the empty seat that had been left for him in front of the men. "Just here on my time."

"I take it you're ready to discuss the plan," the one next to the middle one said.

"I sure am," he said with a grin. "I told y'all I don't wanna be under my cousins' wing anymore. I wanna do shit on my own. So tell me how you all plan to make me richer than I already am."

CHAPTER 6

$\mathcal{T}$oday had been a chill Saturday for Kisan, and right now he was completely focused on the conversation he was having via text with Lucas. Luciana was currently having a nap, so Kisan was alone, and as for Dazhanae, she'd left early this morning to buy groceries, and Kisan was anxiously awaiting her return.

Lucas: *I honestly just wanna go back to NYC. This place just ain't for me anymore.*

Kisan: *Huh? Nigga, you just got back.*

Lucas: *And I'm ready to go again. Like honestly, NYC is my home now.*

Kisan: *I don't like the sound of that shit. Miami used to be your favorite place. Your only home.*

Lucas: *I've built something genuine in NYC with my business though, San. You know I have.*

Kisan: *And why not expand and build it over here too?*

Lucas: *NYC just has my heart now.*

Lucas: *But I hear what you're saying and I'll think about it for sure.*

Lucas: *How are you though?*

Kisan: *Pissed the fuck off.*

Kisan: *I found out Dazhanae told Lu to tell me to stay around more.*

Kisan: *All this time I thought it was something Lu wanted but it was just for Dazhanae's benefit.*

Lucas: *Damn, she's sneaky. Have you told Solána?*

Kisan: *I haven't seen her since that day in my office when she burst in and we fucked.*

Lucas: *In the office?*

Kisan: *Yup. Window wall.*

Lucas: *Against the office window?*

Lucas: *Nigga you really are a freak.*

Kisan: *Man whatever. Shit happened, and it was bomb.*

Lucas: *So y'all getting back together? When was the last time you hit her up?*

Kisan: *I haven't.*

Lucas: *What?*

Kisan: *I ain't hit her up.*

Lucas: *Why?*

Kisan: *Shit's just so messed up since I broke up with her.*

Lucas: *Notice the keyword 'I'. She never ended things. You did, nigga. Because of Luciana who you just said didn't actually want to say the shit she said. Baby momma made her, remember?*

Kisan: *Yeah, matter fact I hear her stupid ass coming through the door right now and I need to check her on that bullshit she put Lu up to.*

Kisan: *Holla at you later nigga.*

Lucas: *A'ight. Don't kill her.*

"Hey, baby."

I'ma try not to, Kisan typed back before locking his phone, dropping it on the counter and looking ahead at Dazhanae who had just entered the kitchen with groceries.

"Don't 'baby' me," he snapped, glaring at her with irritation. "I know what you did."

Dazhanae's heart skipped a beat at his words, and she could feel her body slowly begin to shake.

"W-What do you mean?" she nervously asked, dropping the bags onto the marble counter.

"Don't play with me, Dazhanae." The serious look in his eyes only made her nerves build faster. "I know what you put Lu up to. Using her to guilt trip a nigga into staying around not for her benefit but for yours."

A light sigh of relief released from Dazhanae's lips. She had thought that April had revealed to Khaleeq that drunken night between them. Thankfully, she hadn't, which meant that April was still patiently waiting for her to complete the DNA test.

"You must be retarded as fuck, using my daughter for your personal gain and..."

Kisan was going off on her at this point, but Dazhanae had completely zoned out. She'd almost fainted on the spot thinking that Kisan had found out the truth about Luciana not being his. A truth that he couldn't ever find out. Dazhanae didn't care whatever she had to do to ensure that he didn't find out, but she would do it. This was a secret that she was taking with her to the grave.

"You try that foul shit again, and I promise you it'll be the last thing you ever do."

Dazhanae said nothing in return to his concluding sentence, and that only angered Kisan further.

"You hear what the fuck I just said?"

"Yes," she quickly responded. "It won't happen again. I'm sorry."

Because of Dazhanae's sneaky ways, Kisan had messed up something really good with Solána. She didn't even know about Solána, but Kisan knew that Dazhanae wasn't dumb. Knowing that Kisan rarely slept with her was proof enough that somebody else was in the picture. Kisan knew that he needed to fix things with Solána. The question was how?

"So how are my favorite ladies in the whole wide world?" Carolina asked the trio who sat comfortably on her beige couches. She had just walked into the living room with a tray of drinks for them.

"I feel dead inside every day," Sabrina mumbled before reaching up for her drink and grabbing it from the tray that had come her way. "Thank you."

"Dead inside?" Monalisa gave her a strange look before grabbing her glass from the tray and thanking her auntie. "Why you gotta be so dramatic though?"

"Mona," Caroline called her. "Your sister's going through a rough time; let her be as dramatic as she wants."

"I know, but she's moving on with the man she chose. Troy. So how is she still feeling dead inside when she's chosen to lie in the bed she made?"

"I didn't choose him," Sabrina chimed in. "I'm settling with him though because I don't want him to do something stupid."

"I don't think he tried to commit suicide," Solána revealed, grabbing her glass and also thanking her auntie. "I think he's only saying that to guilt trip you. It's manipulative, and it's working, Rina. You're only staying with him out of guilt for what you did and hurting Kadeem."

"I completely agree," Monalisa said after sipping her drink before placing it down on the coffee table opposite her. "You don't love him the way you love Kadeem."

"What Kadeem and I have is over though. He made that fully clear."

"But just because what you and Kadeem have is over, doesn't mean that you need to settle for a man you don't want, sweetheart. You know in your heart you don't want Troy, and even though what you did with him was wrong, I believe it's helped you realize that you don't want him anymore," Carolina explained with a comforting look as she took the empty seat next to Sabrina. "Don't force yourself to do something that you don't want to do."

All Sabrina could do was sigh and nod at her aunt, no longer in the mood to be talking about her depressing situation. Everything about her situation she loathed, and talking about it just didn't help in any shape or form.

Carolina watched her nieces with a happy smile, glad to be spending the day with them. She paid extra attention to Monalisa, noticing her constant glances to her phone and the small smile that grew on her lips. She could tell that Mona had met someone, but she wasn't about to put her on the spot about it just yet. Carolina would allow her to come talk to her in her own time.

As Carolina continued to stare at the trio, her nerves grew. Suddenly, she had an urge to tell them what had been bothering her for the past few weeks. Keeping this secret from them wasn't something she was sure she would be able to do anymore.

Just tell them.

The more Carolina thought about doing it, the more fear clouded her thoughts and discouraged her. Telling them was much easier said than done.

Where would she even begin?

This secret had been kept buried from them their whole lives, and to uncover it now would be catastrophic. Absolutely catastrophic.

I need to talk to him and see if I can convince him to just leave it alone. He can't say anything. He just can't.

Carolina knew what she needed to do. She had made her mind up about the matter. The girls could never find out the truth.

~ Hours Later ~

How she'd even made it on a second date with Blake was beyond her. But she was happy to know that no one was interfering, and she could freely get to know Blake.

"How's your painting coming along?" he asked her with a curious stare embedded in his brown eyes. "Mine's rubbish."

Solána smirked before taking a sip of her red wine and glancing back down at her painting. It was her first ever attempt at painting a red rose, and for a beginner, it didn't look too bad.

"It's actually coming along okay," she replied, placing her glass down. "I didn't even know I could paint."

"You weren't an artist in school?"

"Hell no," Solána voiced with a scoff. "I could never pay attention when it came to art."

Blake had booked a painting class for them to join while drinking red wine. It was something different yet fun, and Solána greatly appreciated the effort he was making in getting to know her.

"Really? I find that strange, especially with how amazing your store is."

He'd even paid her a visit one afternoon at her store, eager to check it out. His compliments had gassed her up completely, and she found herself smitten by him. Getting to know Blake was like a breath of fresh air, especially with all she'd been through. She really wasn't sure if she liked him enough to be in a real serious relationship with him, but she liked him enough to keep on dating him and getting to know him.

From their first date, she'd learned that he was a banker and had moved to Miami to help partner and invest in his friend's business. He was a British native, born and raised in West London by his mom and dad.

"So what are your thoughts on me seeing you again?"

Solána watched him closely, surprised by his question. Their painting class was over, and now they were standing in the parking lot of where their cars were parked side by side. He stood opposite her, leaning against his car while she did the same, leaning against her car.

"You want to see me again?"

"Of course I do, Solána. I don't want to stop seeing you."

Lowkey, Solána wished that Kisan would make an appearance on one of her dates. But he didn't. And that told Solána all she needed to know about how he felt about her. So she wasn't going to stop seeing Blake. It was time to move on the same way Kisan had.

"I don't want to stop seeing you either."

CHAPTER 7

onalisa continued to push her cart through the store, scanning the shelves for pasta. Her urge to cook mac and cheese had come on strong, and she was determined to make a fresh batch today.

Ding!

Feeling her phone vibrate in her back pocket made her reach for it and bring it out.

I haven't eaten anything yet, Mo.

Monalisa: *Well you better fix that.*

Khaleeq: *Why can't you? You said you're grocery shopping, right?*

Monalisa: *Yup.*

Monalisa had her phone in hand and her other hand pushing the cart along as she continued looking for her pasta. Finally, she found it and placed it in her cart.

Khaleeq: *Then you can fix that.*

Monalisa: *You don't need me to fix you something, Leeq. You're always eating good.*

Khaleeq: *I'm not eating good until you're on my tongue.*

Monalisa couldn't help but blush at his message before responding, *Real smooth mister.*

Khaleeq: *Coming to see you later.*

Khaleeq: *And I'll show you just how smooth I really am.*

Monalisa continued to blush at his text, feeling butterflies grow in her stomach at the thought of seeing him again.

Monalisa: *Sounds good.*

Khaleeq: *Just good?*

Monalisa: *Perfect.*

Khaleeq: *That's more like it.*

Khaleeq's wedding was just under three weeks. The more Monalisa tried to push it to the back of her mind, the more it made an appearance and became her whole focus. Things with Khaleeq were complicated, and she knew that the more time they spent with each other, the more her feelings for him grew. Feelings that she'd tried to convince herself were just lust.

Monalisa finished grocery shopping and paid for the rest of her items before making her way to the parking lot. She was eager to get home now more than ever so she could begin fixing up a meal for her and Khaleeq.

Once loading her car with all her items and returning back her shopping cart, Monalisa headed back to her BMW. She was too focused in her own thoughts to notice the car parked next to hers and the man inside it who was carefully watching her. But when he stepped out and called out her name, Monalisa turned around to give him a strange look.

"You know who I am?" she asked, perplexed by how this stranger knew her.

"Yes, I do," he responded coolly.

He seemed to be a friendly looking man. His ebony skin was smooth and even. He had deep set brown eyes that looked awfully familiar to Mona, as if she'd seen them some time before.

The first thought that had come into her head was that maybe he was a potential new client that wanted her to plan his wedding. But his middle age look told her that he wasn't the marrying type.

"Monalisa Claudette Winters."

Monalisa's eyes widened with shock as he announced her full

name. The way he'd said it so freely and comfortably without a care in the world is what shocked her the most.

"H-How do you know my full name?" she queried, worried that she may have had a stalker on her hands.

"I know it because once upon a time, your mother and I were inseparable," he explained, giving her a friendly smile.

"You knew my mother?"

"Monalisa, I know your mother," he explained before adding, "I'm your father."

~ *An Hour Later* ~

Monalisa had returned home, accompanied by the man who claimed to be her father. His name was Romel, and even though she knew that letting a stranger into her home was wrong, something told her deep down in her gut that he wasn't just some stranger.

She made him a cup of coffee before taking a seat on the dining table opposite him. As she stared deeply into his eyes, she didn't know where to begin. Her father was someone that she had never known. He had never been around in her life or her sisters' lives, and she'd always wondered why.

"Why were you never around?" she suddenly asked, watching him take a sip from his coffee.

"Your mom and I... just didn't work out," he said truthfully. "Which was partly my fault but partly..."

When he paused, Monalisa gave him a confused look.

"Partly what?" she queried, intrigued to hear more.

He took a deep breath before responding, "Partly your aunt's fault."

"My aunt? What does she have to do with you walking out on your family?"

"Well for starters," he began firmly. "You can stop calling her your aunt because she's not."

"How can she not be when she's my mother's sis—"

"She's your actual mother, Monalisa."

Monalisa gave him a look of disbelief before speaking up. "When my mom died, she stepped in as our moth—"

He quickly cut her off. "No, that's not what I'm talking about. She's your mother, Monalisa. Your real mother. Not Solána's or Sabrina's, just yours."

Monalisa's face softened at his words. The disbelief that she'd originally felt was now melting away. It had to be because of the seriousness she could see cradled within his chestnut eyes.

"You must be joking."

"I'm not," he affirmed with a straight glance. "And I'm not Solána or Sabrina's father either. I'm just yours."

Monalisa could not believe what this man was revealing. It didn't make any sense to her at all. What did he mean that he wasn't Solána or Sabrina's father? And what did he mean that her auntie was her actual mother? If it was true, then that would mean that Monalisa had been lied to her entire life. Her whole entire twenty-seven years of life.

No way. He must be lying. This makes no sense. Auntie can't be my real mother. She just can't be. I had a mother and she died.

Romel elaborated further, and Monalisa found herself teary eyed as the truth was exposed.

Carolina had met Romel, aged twenty-eight. At first, things were perfect between them. They went on dates and got to know each other, but a year into their relationship, things turned sour really quick. Romel lost his well-paid job and was unable to spoil Carolina and take her out like he usually would. Carolina started to resent him and hardly made the effort to see him. Then one day, she came to his home telling him that she had found out she was pregnant. He was excited to be a father until Carolina told him that she was getting an abortion and wanted nothing more to do with him.

She claimed that her parents would disown her for having a child out of wedlock, and especially for having a child with a broke man. It hurt him to know that she was willing to abort their child, but he knew he couldn't force her to do anything she didn't want to do.

Years later, Romel had moved on with his life, and he had become the CEO of a successful clothing brand. But the one person who still remained in his head after all these years was Carolina. So he set out to find her, failing to do so, but finding her sister instead, Kamele Winters.

Finding her and telling her who he was turned out to be a bad experience because she seemed to hate him without even truly knowing him. Once finally trying to convince her of his genuine nature, she revealed all to him. How Carolina had told her that he had raped her one night and how afraid she was to have an abortion. Keeping the baby was the only thing she could do. However, she didn't want to lose her parents' respect because they were really strict on marriage and babies. If any of the sisters had a child out of wedlock, they would be disowned straight away.

So Carolina asked Kamele to take her child after its birth and raise it as her own with her husband. Kamele had been trying for months to have a baby and still wasn't pregnant. Therefore, Kamele raising Monalisa was a perfect idea. Kamele raised Monalisa as her own and had Solána a few years later followed by Sabrina, and the rest was history. The only thing was just before Sabrina had turned one, Kamele's husband had walked out on them all, leaving Kamele as a single mother. Carolina was too busy living it up and traveling the world with various wealthy bachelors that desired her. Too busy to come back home to her sister, her nieces, and her daughter.

Romel told Kamele his side of the story and what Carolina had told him about the pregnancy. He hadn't even found out about Monalisa's existence until Kamele had revealed it, and now that he knew, he was gutted; gutted that he had been robbed of getting to know his daughter. He wanted to stay and get to know her, but deep down, he knew he couldn't. He'd built a life in Atlanta; a life that Monalisa wouldn't be happy in. She didn't even know who he was, and Romel felt it was best that it stayed like that.

"I see now that leaving you was wrong," he announced truthfully. "I should have gotten to know you, but you were so young and innocent, and you loved your cousins... your sisters. I didn't want to take you away from them."

An endless stream of tears was flowing down Monalisa's cheeks. At this point, she felt like she wanted to die. Dying would be better than this constant heartbreak she could feel deep inside, all because her mother had decided to keep this secret from her.

"But I'm here now, Mona... and I want to be in your life. I know it's late, but better late than never. I'm getting old, and one day I won't be here anymore, but I didn't want to regret not telling you who I really was," he explained wholeheartedly, reaching for her hand across the dining table.

"B-But why now?" Monalisa asked shakily. "Why would you come into my life after all these years?"

"Because I wouldn't be able to live with myself knowing that the only child I have in this world thinks I was some deadbeat dad that didn't care. Because believe me, I did."

Monalisa removed her hand from his and used it to wipe away her tears. This pain in the center of her chest was a pain that she desperately wished she could get rid of.

"And like I said, I'm getting old, Mona, and soon I'll no longer be able to run my company. I want you to be able to take over it. I want you to take over it and use it to build your wedding company even bigger than it is now."

Monalisa gave him a surprised look. "You know about my company?"

"Yes," he said with a nod. "I Googled you. I know about the wedding planning, your cake company, and I'm so proud of you, sweetheart. I really am. And I want to make sure that you get everything you deserve in this life. Once you inherit my company, you'll become a millionaire. I can tell you love working, but if you choose to ever stop, you can be rest assured that you won't need to work ever again and have all the financial freedom you need."

This was all too much for Monalisa. Truths had been brought to the light, but most importantly, Monalisa felt like her heart had been ripped out of her chest. Solána and Sabrina were not her real sisters. They were her cousins, and more than ever, Monalisa felt betrayal.

Betrayal from the one person that she thought she could trust with her entire life.

Her mother.

Monalisa knew that the one thing she needed to do was confront Carolina. She needed to hear what her father had told her directly from Carolina. A small part of her was hoping that Carolina could convince her that Romel was mad and that this was all a lie. One big fat lie.

"ARE YOU MY REAL MOTHER?"

Monalisa gave her a firm stare, trying to make sure that she could read the answer in her eyes before she spoke. When her eyes started blinking rapidly and filled with tears, Monalisa knew that everything Romel had said was true.

"Twenty-seven years!" Monalisa yelled at her furiously. "You've lied to me for twenty-seven years!"

"Mona, I never meant to hurt y—"

"Well guess what? That's exactly what you've done! You've lied on my father's name! Let your sister believe that he raped you! How could you be so evil? How could you lie like that? How could you abandon me?"

Monalisa stared at her mother with pure hatred. She didn't care for the tears coming out of her eyes either, because in her mind, they were all crocodile tears. She couldn't believe that she had been lied to her whole entire life.

"I hate you."

"No, Mona. Please don't say that," Carolina pleaded, sauntering closer to her, only for Monalisa to step back. "Monalisa, please, just let me explain."

"Don't come near me," she snapped, cutting her eyes at her. "You've smiled in my face this whole time, letting me believe that Solána and Sabrina were my sisters and that you were my aunt! What is there to explain? You've been nothing but a liar, and I will never forgive you for this!"

"Mona, I couldn't say anything because I knew how bad it all looked. I didn't want to ruin our relation—"

"Well congratulations! You've ruined our relationship, and you've ruined my life!"

"If I could go back in time and change things, I swear I would."

"You can't though! You can't change shit about this situation! You can't fix this, and I'll forever hate you because of what you've done. I'll never forgive you," she concluded coldly, giving Carolina one last glance before storming out of her home.

"Mona, please don't g—"

Slam!

Monalisa slammed shut the door behind her and didn't bother looking back. She didn't care how harsh her words sounded. They were the truth. She wasn't sure if she was going to be able to ever bounce from this. How could she? How could she ever look Carolina in the eyes again with love and care? How would she be able to look at her sisters knowing that they weren't even her real sisters? They were only cousins.

"I don't even know what to say..."

Monalisa gently cried into his chest, hating this heartache that remained deep within her.

"I'm so sorry, Mo," he whispered, wiping her tears away with his hand and kissing her forehead.

She kept her eyes shut, hoping that it would stop her tears, but it didn't. They were coming whether she wanted them to or not. Khaleeq being here to keep her company after her traumatizing day was heartening to say the least. But deep down, Mona knew that having him here was nothing but wrong. He was getting married to someone else in a few weeks, not her.

"Khaleeq," she called out his name, lifting her head up from his chest and opening her teary eyes. "What are we doing?"

He glanced carefully at her before sighing softly at her question. That dreaded question that he'd tried to ignore for the past few weeks that he had spent between her thighs.

What are we doing?

Khaleeq had proposed to someone else. April. She was the woman that he would be walking down the aisle with. Not Monalisa. So what were they doing? He couldn't deny that there was a spark with Monalisa that he hadn't felt in an awful while. A spark that was intoxicating, and he never wanted to stop experiencing it. But how could he be intoxicated with the woman that he hadn't even known for very long? The woman that had come into his life to help him plan his wedding?

What were they doing?

The sex had been undeniably amazing. Both of them knew that for sure. But even just being able to be in each other's companies was amazing too. They got along extremely well. Too well.

"What are we doing?" he repeated after her. "I don't even know."

Monalisa felt her heart sink at his words. She didn't know what she was expecting him to say, but it wasn't that.

"You're getting married to April," she reminded him.

"I am."

"So I think that's what you need to focus on," she said.

"You're right," he agreed with her reluctantly. "I do need to focus on that."

She gave him a weak smile before shifting away from him on the bed.

Khaleeq took this as his signal to go. It was clear from her statements and sure facial expressions that she was ending what they had started. And he would have to accept that they could never be anything more. He was getting married to April, and his priority needed to be realigned with her in mind. But a small part of him wanted to tell Monalisa to shut up and keep her in his arms while comforting her through this dreadful time she was going through. He wanted to be there for her. He wanted to be her man. However, he belonged to someone else.

~

"WHERE WOULD you like to go on your next date?"

Solána stared into her bright screen, admiring how good Blake looked on FaceTime in the mornings. Surprisingly, he had decided to start a FaceTime call with her, and at first, she was a little bit afraid of him seeing her so early in the day, but then she figured, why not?

"Hmmm, let me think," she announced blissfully. "I don't really mind, surprise me."

"Surprise you?" he asked, raising a brow at her. "You're sure about that?"

"Oh, absolutely." She cracked a small smile. "I want you to surprise me. No pressure though."

"No pressure? I feel like I'm going to have to bring my A game to this third date, or you're going to hate it... Hey, what's so funny?" he queried, noticing the amusing expression plastered on her face.

"It's just your accent," she admitted with a light giggle. "It really is the cutest thing ever."

"Well I'm glad I make you laugh, sweetheart."

"I'm glad you do too," she responded, climbing out of bed and heading through her bedroom to the door. She kept her eyes focused on her phone as she sauntered through her living room and headed to the kitchen on the other side. "So what are your plans for today?"

"Work, work, and more work," he said with a deep sigh. "I'd rather have other plans though."

Solána kept her eyes glued on his, a smirk plastered on her lips while entering her kitchen and walking straight to her silver fridge.

"Oh really? And what would that be?"

The cold air hit her face as she opened her fridge, scanning her shelves for her breakfast smoothie.

"Going someplace romantic," he announced confidently. "With a gorgeous girl."

"She sounds like a very lucky girl indeed," she responded, shutting her fridge and turning around to lean against her marble counter with her smoothie in hand. "And where exactly is this romantic pl…"

Solána's words immediately trailed off and she found her breathing come to a halt when she spotted the tall, handsome figure dressed in all black, who was leaning against her kitchen wall.

Oh. My. God.

"Solána? What's wrong? You look like you've just seen a ghost."

Blake's voice suddenly sounded like a distant whisper. *How long has he been standing there for? Why the hell didn't I notice him before?*

"B-B-Blake, I'm gonna have to call you back."

"No you won't be calling anybody the fuck back," Kisan finally spoke up, his eyes shooting daggers her way. "Especially not that stupid lil' white boy you've been goofing around with. So end that mothafuckin' call before I end him, then you."

CHAPTER 8

*S*ilence.

The quietest yet loudest noise of them all. And right now, between Solána and Kisan, silence was the loudest thing in the room. She stood by the kitchen counter while he stood by the sink.

She refused to look at him, and that crushed him. He hated when she did that shit, and now that she was doing it, he wanted to shoot someone. The white boy that she had been going out with behind his back was the first person on his hit list.

"Do me a favor real quick. Open the fridge behind you," Kisan finally spoke up calmly.

Solána gave him a baffled look, keeping her arms crossed in front of her.

"Sorry?"

"You heard me."

"I did, but you're not making any sense, Kisan. You break into my home, and now you're asking me to open my fridge."

"Just go into your fridge, and look for something real quick," he simply said, gazing at her intensely.

Solána sighed softly, turning around to pull her silver fridge handle.

"And what would that something be?"

"You lookin' inside the fridge, right? It should be in there."

Solána's eyes scanned her fridge's shelves and compartments. She didn't see anything out of the ordinary which is why she felt more confused at Kisan's request.

"What should be in here, Kisan?"

"Your damn mothafuckin' mind," he snapped. "Because clearly you've fuckin' lost it. That's why you've been acting like a dumb ass."

Solána felt her blood begin to boil, and she quickly shut her fridge before turning to face him.

"That lil' white boy," Kisan said plainly. "You ain't seeing him no more."

Seeing the nasty glare appear on her pretty face, angered him further.

"And you better wipe that stupid look off your face 'cause I'm not fuckin' playing with you, Solána."

"You can't make me do anything," she countered, crossing her arms across her chest. "Blake and I are getting to know each other and like each other very much."

"Oh, is that right?" He chuckled lightly. "So I see what you're trying to do. You're trying to not only get this nigga killed, you're also trying to die." A smirk grew on his lips. "Is that what you want, Solána? You wanna die? You wanna be on the first mothafuckin' flight to heaven? Because believe me, I can make that shit happen if that's what you want."

"What I want is for you to leave me the fuck alone!" she shouted. "You made your decision, so leave me alone! Let me move on!"

"Are you crazy? I'm not letting you give away what belo—"

"I don't belong to you!" she yelled, interrupting him and pointing between her thighs. "This doesn't belong to you anymore! This stopped belonging to you the day you ended us."

"It stopped belonging to me, but you burst into my office and let me fuck the shit out of you 'til you couldn't walk or think straight?"

"So what!" she exclaimed, raising her hands in the air. "I wanted some dick, so I got some dick. Big whoop!"

"So I'm just some dick to you, Solána?" he asked calmly, leaning off the sink and watching her as she rested against her fridge. "I'm just some dick?"

"This is a pointless conversation because we broke u—"

"No, this ain't no mothafuckin' pointless conversation, because I want to hear you say something. I'm just some dick to you?"

She took a deep breath, feeling her frustrations with Kisan heighten, but nonetheless, she answered his question.

"You're not just some dick to me."

"So why the fuck are you acting so stupid? You know exactly who the fuck you belong to, so trying to move on with that fool is something you know you ain't allowed to do. Unless you wanna end up missing, then be my guest."

"How's Luciana, Kisan?"

Kisan's face scrunched up with irritation at her question and her attempt to change the subject.

"Don't do that shit."

"No for real, how is she?" she questioned sincerely. "Because I'm confused as to why you're standing in my kitchen when you should be with the girl that you want to make happy."

Kisan kept silent at her words, so she carried on.

"Breaking into my home? The only person who seems to be acting dumb here is you, Kisan," she boldly stated, but deep down feeling fearful because of the deadly look in his pupils. But she kept on going, determined to get her point across. "You and I are over! Finished! Done! You ended things for your family's sake, so go and be with your family. Stop pulling up on me, and I promise you I will never pull up on you again. What we had is no more. We're no longer together, no longer fucking, which means my pussy is mine! And if I want to give my pussy away, then I will do as I see fit. And there's absolutely nothing you can do to stop me because you don't own me! You never did. So move on, Kisan. Luciana being happy is your main priority, right? So go and be with your main priority, and stop bothering me."

After her announcement, Solána grabbed her smoothie from the kitchen counter and walked right past Kisan.

"Shut my door on your way out, and the next time you break in, I'm calling the cops," she concluded firmly, leaving the kitchen and heading back to her bedroom.

Thinking that he would chase her down and make her listen to what he had to say, Solána prepared herself mentally to deal with his yelling. No yelling came though. Instead she heard his footsteps storm through her home and the slamming of her front door, confirming to her that he had gone.

I just turned, just turned down your avenue
I had to but I'm mad at you
You always say I gotta attitude

Solána lifted her hand and saw her sister's caller ID appear on her phone's screen. She immediately picked up.

"Rina… what's up?… Now? What's happened?… Alright, I'm on my way."

An hour and a half later, Solána had gotten dressed and had arrived at her aunt's house. She didn't know what was going on. She had simply been told by Sabrina that there was an emergency and their aunt needed to see them now.

"Auntie, what's going on?"

From the tense look her aunt had, Solána could tell that whatever was going on was serious. She glanced at Sabrina who glanced back at her and shrugged.

"And where's Monalisa?"

Her aunt released a deep sigh before deciding to address the elephant in the room. "Monalisa won't be here because she's already found out what I'm about to tell you both."

Both Solána and Sabrina kept their eyes glued on their aunt as they anxiously waited for her to reveal what was wrong. Carolina took a deep breath and then revealed it all.

"I am Monalisa's real mother. I've kept that from the three of you, but I can no longer do that because Monalisa's father wants to be back in her life. He never knew about her until your mother, my sister, told

68

him and showed her to him. I was selfish back then because I broke up with him because he lost his job and was unable to continue spoiling me with expensive gifts and clothes. I told him about the pregnancy but said that I was getting an abortion and could never bring a child out of wedlock because my parents would disown me. I lied about the abortion, but I wasn't lying about my parents disowning me. That's why I looked to your mother for help. I was too afraid to have an abortion, and she had been struggling to have a child. I also lied on Monalisa's father's name and told your mother that he raped me. I just wanted her to feel more sympathy for me and take Monalisa. And it worked. After I gave birth, your mother took her in as her own. Then a few years later, you came along, Sol, then you, Rina."

Solána and Sabrina couldn't believe the words that had come out of her mouth. Sabrina instantly burst into tears whereas Solána just stared at Carolina with a scornful look. She wasn't emotional, just angry.

"You've allowed us to believe for our whole lives that Monalisa is our sister. You've been lying to her, and all this time, you've been her mother? You couldn't even have the decency to tell Monalisa that her mother is still alive and well! You carried her for nine months and gave her up! You manipulated our mother into raising your child and never once thought to help her or, better yet, take your child back. How wicked could you be?"

Carolina's tears started sliding down her cheeks, and her silence drowned her. She couldn't bring herself to speak anymore because she was completely distraught and ashamed about this whole situation. And seeing Sabrina cry was only breaking her heart further.

She had ruined their lives.

~ A Few Days Later ~

One thing Monalisa was never going to do was allow her personal life to stop her from securing her coins. Her company was her pride and joy, and the only thing that could cheer her up from her problems.

She'd ignored the calls and texts from her cousins because she wasn't ready to face them yet. She knew that they knew because they both kept apologizing in their messages to her. Why they kept apologizing, Mona just didn't understand. This wasn't their fault at all. It was her mother's.

Her father had hit her up a few times too, but she'd told him that she needed some space and time to get over the whole situation. When she was ready to talk to him, she would let him know.

"I really can't believe it's two weeks away," April commented blissfully. "I'm really getting married."

Today April had called Mona over to her house to make sure that all the details for the wedding had been finalized. Khaleeq was home, but Monalisa hadn't caught a glimpse of him, and she was praying it stayed like that. She really wasn't trying to see him.

"You really are," Monalisa responded, giving her a small smile. "You must be so excited."

"Excited, but nervous as well," April admitted. "What if something goes wrong? What if he changes his mind and decides he doesn't want me anymore?"

"No, I'm sure nothing will go wrong," Monalisa said, assuring her with a smile. "You love him. He loves you. That's why you're getting married."

"You're right. You're right."

"And we've planned a perfect wedding, so stop worrying. Everything's gonna be fine," Monalisa promised. "We've gone over all the details. Is there anything else you need from me?"

"No, I don't believe there is," April replied. "But I really do want to show you my dress before you go."

Monalisa willingly nodded, honored that April wanted to show her wedding dress.

"Great! Let me just run upstairs and get it. I'll be right back," she stated before getting up from the dining table and leaving Monalisa alone.

Monalisa sighed deeply, running her hand across her face. She was just praying that seeing this dress happened quickly so that she could leave.

"Mona."

Hearing his deep voice startled her, and she looked up to see him walking into the dining room. She hated how good he looked right now in black basketball shorts and a loose black short sleeved top. His muscles were out, and they greatly enticed her, but she quickly snapped out of it remembering where she was and who was upstairs.

"Khaleeq, she's upst—"

"Upstairs, I know," he finished off her sentence for her. "I just wanted to see you before you left."

Mona exhaled lightly and remained silent. She didn't know what to say to him.

"Mona, I'm gonna make this quick," he said as he stopped by the table she was sitting at. "I have feelings for you. I've tried my hardest to get you out my head, and I just fuckin' can't, Mo. I can't stop thinking about you, and I know how complicated this shit is, but I can't help how I feel."

As smitten as she was by his words, Monalisa was worried that April was about to return at any moment.

"Khaleeq, April could come i—"

"And I don't really give a fuck," he snapped, reaching for her hand and gently pulling her out of her seat. "I want you."

"You're getting married," she whispered, letting him hold her hand with one hand and using his other to grab her waist. "To the woman that you love. Not m—"

Before she could finish her sentence, Khaleeq branded their lips together and kissed her passionately. Meshing their tongues together in perfect harmony. Mona didn't bother fighting the kiss because she wanted it. She wanted this man badly despite knowing that he wasn't hers to want.

"Kha... Kha... Apr... mmh, Leeq."

Khaleeq ignored her protests and continued tonguing her down, completely not caring that his fiancée was upstairs and could enter at any moment.

~

APRIL HAD BEEN PULLING her wedding dress out of her wardrobe when she felt her phone vibrating in her back pocket. Pulling it out and seeing Dazhanae's name appear made her quickly pick up.

"Dazhanae, have you done the test?"

"Is that any way to greet your friend?" Dazhanae fired back.

"Oh, I'm sorry," April apologized sarcastically. "Hi, Dazhanae. How are you today? Have you done the test?"

"I'm working on it."

"That's not good enough."

"What do you expect me to do now that Kisan doesn't spend the night anymore? He only focuses on Luciana then he's gone."

"Well I'm sure you'll think of something. I really need to go now, Dazhanae. I've got my wedding planner downstairs. You know what you need to do. So hurry before I lose my patience and tell Khaleeq. You have until my wedding."

"No, Apri—"

Before Dazhanae could get another word in, April hung up and placed her phone back in her pocket. Then she picked up her dress, folding it into two and carrying it while she headed back downstairs to Monalisa, only to enter the room with surprise at what she could see.

"Leeq, baby, I thought you were busy?"

Khaleeq was standing by the dining table while Monalisa remained seated.

"Oh. I just came to holla at Mo…na real quick."

April had now hidden her dress behind her back and had a sneaky grin on her face.

"Monalisa, let's go somewhere else so I can show you my dress before you go. Leeq, baby, you know it's bad luck for the groom to see the dress before the wedding, so you can't see it."

April stepped backward, exiting the room in a way that ensured that Khaleeq couldn't see her dress. But the joke was on her, because he had already seen it one night in her wardrobe.

Monalisa quickly got up from her seat ready to follow April out until she felt her waist being grabbed. She turned around, and that's when she felt his lips on hers once more. He tightly squeezed her butt and kissed her deeply. Then she placed a hand on his chest and pushed him back. He smirked at her and watched a shy smile appear on her lips.

"Mona?" April's head quickly popped back into the room to see Monalisa casually walking toward her.

"Right behind you."

CHAPTER 9

"*D*amn, I ain't beaten your ass in a minute. I almost forgot how good I am at this shit," Kisan commented happily as he kept his focus on the large plasma screen ahead; the screen that had the street fighter game he was playing at his crib with Lucas.

"Man, shut up. I'ma beat your ass in a hot minute; just you wait and see," Lucas promised, clicking away on his controller while his eyes remained locked on the screen.

"Ain't gonna happen," Kisan boasted while effortlessly beating up Lucas's character.

"Oh, come on!" Lucas shouted in protest.

Ding!

Kisan took his eyes off the screen for a second to look at his flashing phone. It turned out to be an Instagram notification telling him that Solána had just posted a new picture. He immediately paused the game and unlocked his phone, eager to see what she had posted.

"Nigga, what the… Kisan."

"What?" he asked, his eyes fixed on his screen. "For fuck's sake, this girl keeps playing with her life."

Without even needing to see what Kisan was looking at, Lucas knew he was on Solána's Instagram page.

"Bro, you need to let her go. You haven't made any effort to get back with her, and now you keep stalking her page and shit like some psycho."

"She's fuckin' posting captions about that clown all the time, and you expect me not to care?"

"No one's saying you can't care. I'm just saying you haven't really done anything about it."

"I was going to," he said with a sigh, chucking his phone to the side of the couch. "But she said some shit that made me want to leave her alone. I told you what she said, and I haven't talked to her since."

"She basically reminded you of your reasons for breaking up with her. Reasons that are no longer valid because you found out that they didn't even come from Luciana," Lucas stated. "So the only person stopping yourself from getting back with her is you."

"I don't even know how to get her back. Now that I know she's dating, I'm angry as hell at her. I miss her so fucking much, but to see her actually move on is irritating," Kisan admitted with a stressed look. "I want her back, but where do I even start? I've messed up bad, and I don't think she wants anything to do with me anymore. She straight up told me to leave her alone and get the hell out her crib."

"But you love her, right? And we both know that just 'cause she said some shit, doesn't mean you're going to leave her alone. You know she loves you too, so fighting for her is just something you're going to have to be prepared to do. Fight for the woman you love."

"But if I do all this fighting and it only pushes her further away, I've lost her for good, Lucas. I don't want to lose my baby."

"Be straight up and honest with her. Admit your wrong doings, but make it clear that you want her. Make it clear that you love her."

Kisan contemplated about Lucas's advice. His last line really stuck to Kisan because he knew that's exactly what he needed to do. He needed to make it clear that he was in love with Solána. He needed to prove to her that he loved her and most importantly he needed to be 100 percent honest with her. It was time to stop messing and win back his peanut.

"You still thinking about heading back to New York?" Kisan queried, wanting to know where his best friend's head was at.

"One hundred percent," Lucas confirmed with a firm head nod, and Kisan knew that he was serious about going back. He didn't want his best friend to go, but he completely understood his reasoning for wanting to go back. He had gotten so comfortable in NYC that Miami just wasn't home for him anymore.

"Whatever you decide to do, just know that I'm with you every step of the way, and I support you 110 percent," Kisan announced in a welcoming and honest tone.

"I really do appreciate that, bro, especially coming from you. I know you gon' miss my ass and be crying every day, but I gotta do what's best for me."

"Whoa, whoa, whoa, whoa," Kisan remarked with a frown. "Nigga, ain't nobody gon' be crying but your ass when you leave me."

Lucas immediately laughed, and the men got back to playing their game while continuing their conversation.

~

"How does that taste?"

Solána carefully chewed on the piece of food in her mouth. Blake had blindfolded her, so she had been unable to see what food had entered her mouth. But now that she could taste and chew on it, she knew exactly what it was.

"Really good, actually," she complimented him, smiling as she kept on chewing on her steak.

"Actually?" Blake asked with a fake hurt look. "So you didn't believe me when I told you I could cook?"

Solána lightly giggled and quickly felt her blindfold being untied. Then it was lifted off her eyes, allowing her to see the empty seat across her. Blake made his way back around and took the seat in front of her.

"It's not even like that; I just wasn't sure," she explained. "But you definitely can cook really well. Thank you for this."

"No worries, love," he said with a gentle smile. "I just wanted to do something nice for you."

Solána froze at his last statement as she reminisced on the last time she had heard someone tell her that.

"Eat up," he ordered, eyeing the tray on her lap. "A nigga slaved away in the kitchen just for you."

He had made her breakfast in bed: pancakes topped with syrup and strawberries, egg, bacon, and sausages. She appreciated the effort he had made this morning. It was a sweet and romantic gesture.

"Thank you, San."

"It's nothing," he voiced. "I just wanted to do something nice for you."

It seemed like no matter how hard she'd tried to push him to the back of her mind, she just couldn't do it. She couldn't forget about him. Trying to act like she didn't love him anymore was a complete failure. He was all she could think about.

"You okay?"

Blake's question made her look up from her plate of remaining food and give him a weak smile.

"You seem like you have a lot on your mind."

"Yeah," she quietly replied. "I do."

"I'm here to listen, so feel free to talk about it," he offered sweetly.

Solána simply nodded and used her fork to poke her food. Talking about Kisan was the last thing she wanted to do because she hated that she couldn't stop thinking about him.

"If you can't stop thinking about him, then do what makes you happy and be with him."

Solána looked up at Blake with a surprised look.

"How did you know?"

"Well for starters," Blake began, "The morning we FaceTimed and you went into the kitchen, I heard his voice."

"Yeah, that was him," Solána confirmed. "I'm sorry, Blake."

"No, don't be. Why are you sorry?"

"'Cause I feel like I've wasted your time when deep down I always knew who had my heart," she explained with a soft sigh.

"Getting to know you has been amazing, and you're a wonderful woman, Solána. All I want is for you to be happy."

"Even if that means me being happy with someone else?" she meekly queried.

"Yeah, absolutely. Your happiness comes first. No one wants to be miserable. To be honest with you, there's someone I've got back home that I can't stop thinking about either."

"So why can't you be with her?"

Blake deeply sighed, reaching for his champagne glass. "Well…" He took a sip before speaking. "Things are just really complicated between us. She's got a lot going on, and I just didn't want to give her any more stress, which is why I moved to Miami without even batting an eyelid. But of course, I miss her."

Solána nodded before answering, "Do what makes you happy, Blake. You want me happy, and I want you happy."

Blake grinned at her joyfully, feeling relieved to have gotten his feelings off his chest. Solána was also relieved but deep down felt guilty for getting to know Blake, knowing that the only man she wanted was Kisan. She was grateful at how sweet and understanding Blake was, and she knew without a doubt they would stay friends.

An hour later, Solána had left Blake's apartment and pulled up to her home, shocked but elated to find Kisan's car parked in her driveway.

When she got out and saw him sitting on the step just outside her door, she wanted to smile but quickly decided against it. Just because she had broken things off with Blake didn't mean that Kisan could immediately worm his way back into her life. After what he had put her through, making her breakdown into a weak individual, she knew that he wasn't going to get an easy route back into her life.

"What are you doing here, Kisan?" she asked, staring at him carefully as he got up in front of her.

"How was your date?" he curiously queried.

"Just fine," she responded with a fake smile. "What are you doing here?"

"I came to see you obviously," he stated calmly, a bit too calmly for

Solána's liking. She expected him to spazz out at the fact that she had come from a date with Blake when Kisan had warned her during their last encounter to stay away from him.

"Why?"

"'Cause I'm sick of this shit, Solána," he snapped with a mean mug. "I'm sick of us doing this."

"Doing what? You were the one that broke up with me; you ca—"

"I made a mistake, Sol! A stupid, fuckin' mistake. I want you back."

"You made a mistake when breaking up with me for Luciana's happiness?" She gave him a curious look.

"I found out that Luciana didn't even really say that shit. It was her mom that put her up to it," he explained with a frown. "Luciana's always understood that her mom and I are not together anymore. She's never had a real issue with it."

"But you were so sure on trying to make things work for her," she reminded him with a firm look. "So what's changed?"

"I fuckin' miss you, Solána!" he yelled. "I'm literally depressed without you in my arms every night and without you being by my side. Solána…" Kisan's words trailed off as he stepped closer to her and lifted a hand to her cheek. "I want you to meet Luciana."

Solána didn't know what to say in response to his words. They were shocking to her without a doubt. He had never asked her to meet Luciana before.

"W-What?"

"I want you to meet Luciana. She deserves to meet the woman that I want to spend the rest of my life with."

Solána continued to stare deeply into his honey brown pupils, still completely shocked by his words.

"I should have never broken up with you, Sol. That was the biggest mistake of my life, and I promise I'll never do it again. I never want to lose you again, peanut. I was a fool to let you go the first time, and I'll be a fool to let you go again. I'm sorry, baby." He gently pecked her lips. "Please forgive me. Whatever a nigga gotta do to make things right, I'll do."

Solána could feel her nerves building as they stayed standing in front of each other. Despite the nerves she could feel, her happiness was undeniable. Standing here with Kisan felt amazing. It was great to hear him admit his faults and work on making things up to her. And it was especially great to have him exactly where she needed him to be: desperate and weak for her to take him back.

"You've said a whole lot of sweet shit, Kisan. But what you've come to say today changes nothing," Solána announced, removing his hand from her cheek and stepping back from him.

"What?" He looked at her with confusion. "What do you mean?"

"We're not getting back together," she affirmed, crossing her arms in front of her chest.

"The fuck you mean we not getting back together? I just poured out my heart to you, Solána."

"And give yourself a big round of applause because that was an excellent performance you just put on," she said smugly. "You think coming to my doorstep, apologizing and trying to get me to meet Luciana is going to change what you did to me?"

The loving look in his eyes had instantly changed to deadly. "Solána, how many times do I need to say I'm fuckin' so—"

"As many times as you like," she stated coolly. "The day you broke up with me, you broke me, Kisan. You turned me into a woman that I've never been. You made me feel like shit, and all I kept thinking was how I couldn't live without you. I was weak in every single part of my body, and I can't believe that you got me like that. I see now that the fact that you think you can just waltz up in here and say sorry shows how truly crazy you are. I couldn't sleep, Kisan!" she yelled, feeling her eyes water up. "I couldn't eat. I couldn't wash myself for weeks! Because of you! Because you had broken my heart!"

Kisan remained silent, his breathing increasing with each passing second because of how pissed he was. Pissed that she wouldn't accept his apology, and pissed at himself for being stupid enough to end things with her and break her heart.

"You can't just decide to play with my emotions as you see fit. What you did was wrong, and I don't think I'll be able to forgive you for that. Ever."

Kisan's eyes widened with alarm at her words. "You're going to punish me for a mistake that I wish I had never made?"

"You punished me when you walked out on me, Kisan. I told you that I loved you, and you berated me. You made me feel like loving you was wrong when I knew what I wanted."

"But I love you, Solána! I've always loved you! You know how much I do."

"Kisan, I'm going to need you to let this go."

Kisan had to do a double take to make sure that he wasn't dreaming and hearing things. It sounded like Solána had used the exact same words that he had told her the day he had broken up with her.

"The fuck you just say?" he spat, his face scrunching up with irritation.

"Forget about a nigga," she said, still using his words and giving him a small smile. "You can't love a nigga like me, Kisan."

"Why the fuck are you smiling? You think this shit is fuckin' funny?" he fumed. "Smile at me one more mothafuckin' time, and I promise you, Solána, I promise you I'ma smile in my mugshot tonight. Keep fuckin' playing with me."

She gave him one last glance, ignoring the annoyed and heartbroken look on his handsome face before walking toward her door.

"Solána!" He grabbed her arm and pulled her toward him. "Where the hell do you think you're going?"

"I've said all I need to say to you, Kisan, so this conversation is ov—"

"No the fuck it ain't! It ain't over until I hear you tell me that we're back together."

"I'm not saying it, so keep on dreaming," she responded calmly. "Get off m—"

He held onto her tighter and kept her closer, his pupils piercing into hers. "See this shit right here is what you ain't 'bout to do, Solána, because I promise you this won't end well."

"Is that supposed to be a threat?" she asked with a scoff. "You're even crazier than I thought if you think that you scare me, Kisan."

"I'm going to jail tonight," Kisan commented in a tone that sounded like he was talking to himself rather than her. "This girl is really gon' make me end up in a jail cell."

"Can you get off me please?" She looked down at his hand that was still holding firmly onto her arm. Reluctantly, he let her go.

"Solána, I fuckin' miss you."

"If you acted right, you wouldn't have to."

"Why the hell are you being so difficult? Why the hell are you breaking a nigga's heart right now?"

"Because that's exactly what you did to me," she reminded him calmly. "Now you know exactly how it feels."

And that was the honest truth. Solána knew she was being stubborn, but she had every right to be. She loved this man and couldn't stop thinking about him, but he had hurt her deep; deeper than any man had ever hurt her before.

Kisan could feel his eyes filling with tears, but he held them back as best as he could, watching her closely, praying and hoping that somehow, she would change her mind and forgive him. But she didn't. Instead, Solána walked past him and headed toward her front door. This time, Kisan didn't stop her. He just let her go, knowing that his forceful nature would only drive her further away.

Solána got to her front door, brought out her key, and sighed softly. She knew that Kisan was still standing in the spot she had left him in because she hadn't heard his footsteps walk away yet. So she turned around to see him standing still with his back facing her.

Despite all the pain he had caused her, it was undeniable that she still loved him. The one thing she'd ever wanted was to get back together with him, but now that she had that option, it seemed too attainable for him. And that's the last thing she wanted. If he wanted her back, then he was going to have to be prepared for a challenge.

"Are you sure you want me to meet Luciana?"

Hearing her question made him slowly turn around to face her, and he gave her quick, sure nods, his eyes still watery.

"Alright," she said. "I'll think about it."

After speaking, Solána turned back around, lifted her keys into the lock, and stepped inside her home, exhaling deeply as she shut her door behind her.

THE RESULTS ARE DONE. When do you want them?

Unknown.

Dazhanae sighed with relief knowing that she had managed to fix the predicament that she was in. April had tried to destroy what she had worked so hard to build over the years. She could not let that happen at all. Kisan finding out that his daughter wasn't his could never happen. Dazhanae didn't care what she had to do to ensure that Kisan didn't find out because she was willing to do anything. And whatever she needed to do to get April off her case, she would do.

CHAPTER 10

*M*onalisa had been avoiding her cousins for the longest now. But now that they had shown up on her doorstep, she knew that avoiding them could happen no more. They were adamant on seeing her, and despite her not wanting to talk about the situation, she knew she had to.

"Like, I couldn't even say anything. I burst into tears... I couldn't believe it," Sabrina announced, feeling emotional again.

"I thought it was a joke," Solána chimed in. "But when she kept on going, I knew it wasn't a joke, and this wasn't just some nightmare. This was real."

Monalisa looked from Solána to Sabrina, and seeing the disheartened looks on her cousins faces made her want to break down. She had tried so hard over the last couple of days to keep things together, but now being in their presence was making her want to burst out into tears. And that's exactly what she did, making Sabrina and Solána immediately move onto her couch to each sit next to her. They both reached for her hands and comforted her while she cried.

"Don't cry, Mona," Sabrina gently pleaded, placing her arm around her. "No matter what, we're always going to be sisters. We're always going to have a bond like no other."

Monalisa continued to cry, feeling hopeless and depressed. She still couldn't believe what her mother had done.

"Exactly," Solána intervened. "Mona, just because the truth says one thing doesn't change our truth. All our lives, we've known each other as sisters, and that's what we are. No one will ever be able to come between us and break what we have. No one."

Monalisa nodded in agreement, and her tears slowly slid down her cheeks. She appreciated them both so much, especially because of how supportive they were. She loved them dearly and knew that no matter what, their sisterly bond was forever.

"Let's change the subject please," Monalisa said with a light laugh as she wiped away her tears. "I don't want to cry anymore."

Both Solána and Sabrina nodded in agreement before Solána decided to bring up what had happened last week.

"So Blake realized that there was someone else... and we called things off," she began. "And then Kisan tried to get back together."

"Tried?" Mona asked with a sniffle. "What do you mean?"

"He thought he could just say a bunch of sweet shit, apologize, and then it would all be good. But you both know what he did to me. I can't just let him back in so easy. Can you believe he thought that telling me that he wants me to meet Luciana was going to make everything alright?"

"Awww, that's sweet that he wants you to meet her though," Sabrina chimed in. "But you do want to get back together with him eventually, right?"

"I'm not sure," Solána admitted truthfully.

"You're not?" Monalisa asked. "So why did you end things with fine ass Blake then?"

"'Cause my mind just wasn't in it," she explained. "I don't want to date anyone else."

"You want to date Kisan; yeah, we know," Sabrina said knowingly.

"I just feel like he's gotta earn me back. I don't want him thinking that saying sorry is an easy ride back in."

"He wants you to meet Luciana though," Monalisa reminded her. "So that is definitely a start."

"Do you guys think I should meet her?"

"Without a doubt," Sabrina replied.

"Yes," Monalisa answered with a firm head nod. "He wants you to meet the most important person in his life; this is big for him, and it should be big for you too, Sol."

Solána contemplated about Monalisa's words for a while before speaking up. "I guess it's just something I've got to think about. I mean, I would love to meet his daughter, but I'm a little nervous."

"Don't be," Sabrina stated. "She's just a kid; it's not like she's going to kill you or anything."

Solána chuckled lightly and sighed softly. "Yeah, I'll think about it some more."

"Sounds like a plan. Let us know what you decide," Monalisa requested with a small smile. "And you, Rina? How's things with Troy?"

"Things are... Things are just normal. We're still together, so yeah."

Monalisa nodded, feeling content that her sisters were doing okay and just working through life each day. A small part of her wanted to reveal what was going on with Khaleeq. She was tired of keeping this situation a secret, but she was terrified to tell them because she wasn't sure how they would react to her sleeping with an engaged man; a man that belonged to someone else.

The girls continued to catch up for a few more hours before Solána and Sabrina took their leave. Solána headed home whereas Sabrina didn't. She headed to the one man she wanted to be with despite all the issues and the pain they had put each other through.

Where are you?

Troy.

Sabrina placed her iPhone on do not disturb before locking it and placing it on the lamp stand. Then she turned away from the stand and snuggled back closer to him. He wrapped his arms around her and pulled her even closer.

Sabrina didn't know how it had happened, but she'd found herself back in Kadeem's arms. He had messaged her one night, anxious to see her, and before she knew it, they'd had sex. Now they couldn't stop having sex and seeing each other almost every day.

The tables had truly turned, and Sabrina didn't know what to do about this situation. All she knew was that Kadeem was who she wanted, and she didn't want to stop wanting him.

~ 1 Week Later ~

I want to meet Luciana.
Solána.

He remembered the joy that he had felt seeing her text appear on his screen last week. Knowing that she was finally willing to open up and give him a chance made him feel excited. And to know that the day of her meeting his daughter had finally arrived only made his excitement grow.

"So there's someone that I really want you to meet today, mama," Kisan spoke to Luciana while he drove. She sat in the back seat with her favorite book in her hands.

"Who, dwaddy?"

"My gi..." He was about to say his girlfriend, but then he realized that they weren't even together. "The woman that I'm in love with."

"What's her name?"

"Solána."

"She sounds prwetty," Luciana commented, and Kisan looked through the interior mirror to see her smiling to herself. "Is she prwetty?"

"She's beautiful, mama. Just like you."

Luciana's smile grew larger, and all Kisan found himself doing was smiling at her. He loved how sweet she was being about this situation, and he just honestly couldn't wait to see the look on her face when she met Solána.

Kisan was nervous. He'd tried to suppress his nerves while driving by giving himself a pep talk. *You can do this, nigga. Relax and stop moving like a little bitch.* But he had failed because upon arriving at Solána's doorstep, his nerves had shot through the roof.

"Dwaddy, your hands are sweaty," Luciana said, and he looked down to see her moving her hand out of his.

"Sorry, mama. I'm just ner..." His words trailed off once the front door opened and out the love of his life came.

The smile on her lips brought a glow to her beauty. She didn't seem to have any makeup on, and Kisan absolutely loved that because he hated when she put chemicals on her beautiful skin. She wore denim jeans and a baby pink off the shoulder top with pink Fenty slides on her feet, and her hair was in curls today, cascading around her pretty face. The color pink suited her beautiful chocolate skin well.

"Hello," Solána greeted Luciana, crouching down to her level. "Are those for me?"

Luciana was holding a bouquet of pink roses which evidently matched her top. She nodded and gave them to Solána.

"They match your top," Luciana pointed out happily.

"They do," Solána said with a grin.

"I'm Luciana," she introduced herself. "My dad says you're the woman he loves. Are you?"

Solána's eyes drifted up to stare at Kisan only to wish she lowkey hadn't. Because he looked too attractive, wearing black jeans, a white fitted top and black Hugo Boss sneakers on his feet. He had an optimistic look on his face, and when he offered her a smile, she returned it before looking back at Luciana.

"I am," she answered her. "I'm Solána. My family and friends call me Sol, but you can call me Ana."

Luciana's eyes widened with happiness, and she moved closer to Solána to embrace her, which took Solána by surprise, but she accepted the hug nonetheless.

"My dad says you've got a cat! Is that true?"

"Sure is," Solána confirmed while holding her hand as they walked into her living room together. "Olivia! Liv, baby, come out."

Moments later, Luciana observed as Olivia came out from her hiding spot and sauntered toward her. Kisan was surprised at how big Olivia had grown from when he had seen her last.

Luciana pet Olivia and started to play with her while Solána and Kisan observed with smiles on their faces. Then Solána gave Luciana a drink and a few snacks while they continued to talk to one another. Prior to their arrival, Solána had started preparing a meal for them to all eat together, and it was almost done. Kisan happily watched on as Luciana helped Solána finish off their meal in the kitchen together.

When it was time to eat, they all sat around the dining table, and Solána said grace. While she prayed, all Kisan found himself doing was staring at her. She had her eyes shut, so she couldn't see him looking, but that didn't mean she couldn't sense his eyes glued on her. He couldn't believe that she had allowed him to bring Luciana over. They got along so well, and Kisan just hoped that Solána saw this as him trying to make things right. He knew that he had a whole lot of things left to do, but this was definitely a start.

APRIL HAD her eyes glued on the piece of paper currently in her hands. Dazhanae sat from across her and was watching her intensely, hoping that this would be the final time she had to be in April's presence.

April stayed focused on the results, reading each detail slowly and carefully, not wanting to miss a single piece of information.

"Okay..." April took one last glance over the DNA results before looking up at Dazhanae with a smile. "So he is the father after all."

"I told you," Dazhanae said proudly.

"So why did you say those lies that night?"

"I'd had way too much to drink," Dazhanae explained with a deep sigh. "Yes, I messed around with Lucas, but that was ages ago, and he didn't get me pregnant."

"Yeah, you definitely need to stay away from hard liquor," April informed her tensely. "It's got you out here saying the most random shit. I'm sorry I didn't believe you, but like I said, my loyalty is with Khaleeq and his family always."

"It's cool," Dazhanae said with a shrug. "You did what you had to do. However, I know that our friendship isn't going to be the same after this at all."

April gave her a strange look. "Why not?"

"Because you blackmailed me into doing this, April."

"Only because of my loyalty to Khaleeq! I told you, girl."

"Whatever." Dazhanae dismissed her while getting up from her seat, more than ready to go. "I can't be friends with people who force me into doing things just so that they can feel better about their conscience."

"You were the one that said those things, Dazhanae. What else was I supposed to think? I needed to know the truth."

"You were supposed to trust and believe that Kisan is the father of Luciana. But like I said, it's whatever. I'm just glad this little mishap is sorted. I'll see myself out."

Dazhanae could finally sleep easy at night knowing that Kisan wasn't going to find out the truth about Luciana not being his.

CHAPTER 11

$\mathcal{T}$he day that Khaleeq had thought would never come had finally come. The wedding was tomorrow which meant that he would be married to April in less than twenty-four hours. He had his bachelor party in a few hours with his cousins and close friends then he would be heading to his hotel room.

Marrying April was something that he used to be so certain about, but now he wasn't even sure. Before Monalisa had stepped in, he knew that he wanted to spend the rest of his life with April. Nowadays, he couldn't stand to fall asleep next to her because he'd rather fall asleep with Monalisa in his arms.

How did my life get this complicated? he asked himself as he drove in silence through the streets of Miami. Driving was the only thing that could clear his head right now, so that's what he did. But what was supposed to be a long drive to get a clear mind turned into a drive to Mona's crib. And when he arrived on her doorstep, she let him in with no question.

Now here he stood in her bedroom doorway, observing her pretty face as she sat on the edge of her bed. Silence remained between them, but that was okay because they both understood that today had to be the last night they ever saw each other again.

Khaleeq sauntered toward where she sat, taking the seat next to her and reaching for her hand. He then brought it to his lips, kissing it gently before stroking the top of her hand with his thumb. The feelings that he had for this woman were not disappearing. They were only strengthening and became worse when they were away from each other.

"Khaleeq..." Monalisa looked directly at him, falling deeper in love with those brown eyes of his. Those brown eyes that had reeled her in from their very first encounter.

"Tell me not to marry her and I won't," Khaleeq announced, shocking the both of them.

"W-What?"

"Tell me not to marry her, and I swear I won't," he repeated seriously. "Just say the word, and I won't do it."

Don't marry her, Khaleeq. She could say it in her head, but trying to bring the words out of her mouth just seemed impossible. Monalisa badly wanted to tell him not to marry April. However, it was something she would never be able to do. She had seen the way April looked at him, the way her eyes lit up when she was around him. She had seen the love she had for him, so taking that away from her would crush Monalisa forever. It would haunt her forever.

"You love her, Leeq," she reminded him with a weak smile. "That's why you're marrying her, remember?"

I'm falling in love with you though, he mused, staring silently at her. *I'm in love with you, Monalisa.*

"She's waited so long for this. You've waited so long for this," she continued to speak calmly. "This is the woman you've planned to spend the rest of your life with."

But what if that woman is now you? His private thoughts continued to circulate in his mind, but through it all, he knew that she was right. April was the woman he was getting married to.

Monalisa could feel tears forming in her eyes as she watched him. He looked so lost and confused on what to do, but Monalisa knew that this was it. They could never see each other after today. She leaned in closer to him, pressing her forehead against his before locking lips with him.

When his hands lifted to her cheeks, Mona's tears fell out her eyes. It hurt to know that the man she loved was getting married to someone else. The man that she had loved spending time with, cooking for, laughing with and talking with every day, was not her man.

Their kiss got deeper, and Mona had to quickly pull her lips away from his. She got up from her bed's edge, but Khaleeq only grabbed her waist trying to pull her back next to him.

"Khaleeq, no," she protested, pushing him away. "You need to go. Your bachelor party is in a few hours."

"Fuck that," he snapped. "I want to be with you right now."

"You can't," she said sadly. "We can't do this anymore at all."

"Monalisa, please," he pleaded, getting up from the edge and standing in front of her. She looked up as he towered over her, his tall height turning her on. "Just tell me."

"No," she whispered.

"Please, baby," he begged one last time. "Just tell me not to marry her, and I fuckin' won't. I'll marry you."

Monalisa slowly shook her head at him, her tears sliding down her cheeks again.

"I'll marry you. Right now. Let's go. Wherever you wanna go, we'll go. Vegas? Bali?"

"Khaleeq…"

"Fuck everyone," he fumed, gently grabbing her face. "Say the word, and we'll be on my jet before midnight."

Monalisa continued to cry, looking up at him and feeling her heart break piece by piece. She could see the sincere look in his eyes and knew that he was serious. But she knew that he knew that they could never be together.

"Anywhere you wanna go, I'll go, Mo. I'm dead ass serious. All you gotta do is get a white dress and meet me at the altar."

"No, Khaleeq," she affirmed, removing his hands off her face.

"Marry April. That's the woman you're spending the rest of your life with."

Khaleeq sighed deeply, knowing that Monalisa was right. He was marrying April Jones tomorrow morning, not her.

Khaleeq leaned into her, wanting to give her one last kiss before he went but was stopped when she stepped back. And he knew that from her action it was best he just went. He didn't want to go anywhere though. He wanted to stay right by her side and never leave her. Doing that was much easier said than done though.

He took his leave, getting to her doorway and turning to take one last look at her beautiful face... her beautiful face that was drenched in tears, and all he wanted to do was kiss each one away. Instead, he turned around and walked out her life for good.

"Are you coming back home to me tonight?" Dazhanae questioned Kisan, looking as he opened up Luciana's portrait painting to reveal the hidden safe. He punched in the code and brought out a few stacks of 100-dollar bills then closed the safe. As he shot the portrait closed, he turned to face Dazhanae.

"You know damn well I don't come home to you." He walked over to where she sat and dropped the stacks on her lap.

"What's that supposed to mean?"

"You know, Dazhanae," he fumed. "I don't come home to you, I only come home to Luciana."

"That's not what you say when I'm riding that dick," she smugly said.

"And you haven't rode this dick in weeks," he reminded her. "Your days of riding this dick are over though."

Dazhanae's mouth dropped open.

"I've met someone," he explained, ignoring her shocked look. "And she's the woman that I love and want to spend the rest of my life with. Luciana's already met her, and I know that you'll eventu—"

"Sorry, what?"

"What?" He cut his eyes at her, pissed that she had cut him off.

"Luciana's met her? Without my permission?"

"Don't act crazy," he fumed. "That's my daughter, so whoever I want her to meet, she'll meet."

Dazhanae rolled her eyes at him, making him frown with dismay.

"Roll them eyes back again, and I'll make sure they permanently stay back," he coolly threatened, walking toward the exit.

An hour and a half later, Kisan had dressed up and met up with Kadeem for Khaleeq's bachelor party. Now they were on their way to the strip club that they had rented out tonight for Khaleeq. Kisan was truly proud of Khaleeq settling down and marrying the woman of his dreams. He deserved to turn up tonight because tomorrow he would be tied down forever.

"Drink up, nigga! This is officially your last day as a free man," Kadeem voiced loudly over the booming music of the club as he watched Khaleeq down his tequila shot. He tightly squeezed his shoulders as he watched his cousin take his liquor.

For Khaleeq's bachelor party, his cousins had rented out the entire VIP section of the strip club, Onyx, located in south Miami. They had also hired personal strippers and female waiters who were to tend to Khaleeq the entire night and ensure that he was good. If he needed a lap dance, any second, his strippers would provide him with one. Any drink he required, his waiters would be willing to get it for him; shit, if he needed some head right this instant, the ladies would happily oblige.

"You don't want a dance, Mace?"

Kisan shook his head no at Kadeem's question as he watched the stripper currently backing her ass up on Kadeem. Then he looked to his left to see two bad ass twins twerking on Khaleeq who had a straight face as he watched them perform. For someone getting married tomorrow, he didn't seem excited, and Kisan knew he was going to have to talk to him to see what was up.

Thirty minutes later, Khaleeq had announced that he was heading outside to smoke a blunt, and Kisan took this as the perfect opportunity to talk to his younger cousin.

The night air was cool and somber, providing the perfect vibe for Khaleeq to peacefully smoke some weed. Weed that he'd felt he had needed all day after what he had been through. When he spotted Kisan come out the back door and walk toward him, he took his first hit and inhaled it deeply.

"What's up, Leeq?" Kisan warmly asked, genuinely wanting to know.

"Nothing," he responded, staring into the parking lot where various cars were parked.

"You know better than to lie to me."

Khaleeq sighed before turning to look at Kisan and passing his blunt to him. Kisan willingly took it, lifting it to his lips and inhaling.

"I don't know if I want to marry her," Khaleeq truthfully admitted.

"Why?" Kisan asked, passing the weed back to him as smoke surrounded him. "You never felt like this before."

"'Cause I was sure before, now... shit's just different."

"You love her, right?"

"Yeah," Khaleeq said as he brought the blunt back to his lips. "I do."

"So what's there not to be sure about?"

Once done puffing, he spoke up. "I gotta be honest with you, Mace... I'm in love with someone else."

Kisan gave him a baffled look, wanting him to explain further. "Who the fuck is that?"

"Well, it's someone you know, and honestly, I knew I was attracted to her from the moment I saw her, but I didn't think we would end up messing around. I didn't think I would fall in love with her."

Kisan and Khaleeq had their eyes on each other which meant that they were unfocused on the black sedan that had just pulled into the parking lot.

"You're getting married to April tomorrow though, nigga. How the hell can you be in love with someone else? Who is she anyways?"

"It wasn't intentional at all... it just sorta happened. But it's Mo—"

"Shit, Leeq! LOOK OUT!"

Bang! Bang!

Kisan had been too focused on finding out who his cousin was in love with to even pay attention to the sedan that had pulled up. But when he turned to the parking lot and spotted the car windows rolling down, he knew that someone had come to start some shit. Just as The Williams' brought out their guns from behind their shirts, the guns from the sedan's windows were already shooting. But nonetheless, the cousins took cover, and both shot back, adamant on handling whoever was trying to start some shit.

"Ah, fuck," Khaleeq loudly groaned when he felt a bullet penetrate him.

"Leeq!" Kisan immediately called to his cousin, afraid that he had been hit but still determined on shooting back at the car. "Leeq! You good?"

The black sedan instantly drove off, leaving Kisan and Khaleeq. Kisan quickly ran to his cousin only to look on with horror that he had been shot.

CHAPTER 12

"I'm fine, Unc."

"No you're not fine, son. You could have been killed."

"Well I ain't dead, so can everyone just stop stressing the fuck out," Khaleeq snapped, his irritation heightening.

Kisan had gotten Khaleeq in his car, ready to get him to a hospital when Khaleeq revealed that he wanted to go home. Kisan clearly thought he was crazy because he had an open bullet wound in his shoulder, but Khaleeq was certain that he didn't want to go to a hospital. That only left Kisan with the option of calling their private doctor and taking Khaleeq home.

Luckily, April was at her hotel room tonight so she would not find out about Khaleeq getting shot right this instant. As Khaleeq wanted. He knew how she overreacted about things, and he didn't want her stressing about him getting shot. Thankfully, the bullet had only hit his shoulder and hadn't hit any major veins or arteries. The Williams' private doctor had removed the bullet and bandaged him up. All Khaleeq wanted now was to find who had shot him so he could personally place them in a coffin.

"Is there anything that you boys need to tell me? Any enemies that you've now made that you just happened to not tell me about?" Axel's questions made Kisan contemplate deeply. He had not made any new enemies, and the enemies he did have were all dead.

"Nah," Kisan affirmed with a head shake. "I haven't made any new enemies, and I'm pretty sure these niggas haven't either or else I would know about it."

"So who on earth tried to kill you?" Axel queried, watching the three men intensely. "I'm not gonna rest until whoever did this is found. I want all of you on guard and alert 24/7. I'll have extra men on all of you too."

Khaleeq nodded in agreement before stating, "Well I'm getting married in a few hours, and I need all the sleep I can get right now."

Kisan stared stoically at his cousin as he lay on his king-sized bed. He still didn't know who Khaleeq was in love with because he had been interrupted mid-sentence by the bullets shot their way. And he still wanted to find out. However, it seemed from Khaleeq's comment that he was willing to go down the aisle with April after all, so Kisan would leave him be for now. Maybe the near-death experience was enough to convince him that April was all he needed.

"Alright, we'll leave you to it, son. Rest up; you got a big day ahead of you," Axel concluded with a smile before patting Khaleeq's leg.

"Sorry you got shot, bro," Kadeem stated sympathetically. "We gon' find out who did this though; don't trip."

Khaleeq nodded before looking over at Kisan who gave him a sure look. Kisan was going to make sure that whoever had tried to kill them both would face the consequences of their actions. Trying to come for a Williams was an automatic death wish, and Kisan was willing to grant it to whoever.

Kisan, Kadeem, and Axel had all come up in separate cars, so they said their goodbyes to one another outside of Khaleeq's home and left. Once in his car, Kadeem immediately dialed the number of the person who he was sure was behind this shit. His anger had completely reached overload knowing that The Serbians had tried to kill his cousins.

"What the fuck is wrong with you? That wasn't the plan!... No! You were never supposed to hurt any of them. No! That's not how I said things go... Alright, fuck you then! This shit is done, do you hear me? Don—"

Before Kadeem could get his last few words in, the caller hung up, making him huff and groan in more fury.

~ The Next Morning ~

Sleeping had been a challenge. Monalisa wasn't even sure if she would be able to fall asleep but she had. All she kept thinking about was Khaleeq and the words he had said to her about marrying her instead of April.

I should have told him not to marry her.

Monalisa had woken up, washed, brushed, and gotten dressed into her clothes for April's wedding. However, as she looked in the mirror while putting on her makeup, she quickly burst into tears. This predicament that she was, she just didn't understand. She was supposed to sit and watch the man she loved get married to someone else. How could she do that?

I can't watch him get married.

Why she thought that she would be able to watch him get married in the first place was beyond her. There was no way that she could watch Khaleeq marry April. Even thinking about it brought her to tears, so imagine actually being present at the wedding? It was best that she didn't embarrass herself, and besides, she didn't want to mess up Khaleeq's big day. It wouldn't be fair on him at all.

The only thing she wanted right now was to talk to someone, preferably someone who didn't know about April's wedding today and wouldn't be asking her why she wasn't en-route to the wedding. So she decided to call Romel, her father.

"Monalisa," he greeted her warmly. "How are you?"

She exhaled lightly before replying, "I'm okay. What about you?"

"Good now that I'm on the phone with my daughter," Romel stated. "What do you have planned for today?"

"Well... I was supposed to be on my way to a wedding but... but I'm not feeling too well."

"Oh, that's unfortunate," he voiced sadly. "If you need me to come and be your doctor for the day, don't hesitate to let me know."

Monalisa couldn't help but smile at her father's sweet comment. One thing that Mona knew for sure was that she didn't want to be alone today. And she wanted to see her father. It was time to spend some time getting to know him better and hopefully be able to take her mind off Khaleeq. She'd made up her mind, and she knew for certain that she was not attending the wedding.

"I'd like that very much."

AM I really doing this shit?

Khaleeq stared at his reflection as he his attempted to tie his tie. He was failing miserably though because he couldn't keep his mind off one woman. Monalisa. It sucked to know that his heart was with someone else. He knew that he loved April, but he wasn't in love with her anymore. Not as much as he had now grown to love Monalisa.

It was crazy too, because he hadn't even known her that long. It was only a couple of months, but Khaleeq felt like he had known her forever. Why hadn't he met her before April? If he had met her before then this wouldn't have been an issue and he would be marrying Monalisa instead of April.

But Monalisa hasn't been ride or die like April has, nigga. Come on, you know April would be willing to do anything to make you happy. Khaleeq knew that without a doubt. Whatever he wanted, April provided it. She stood by him through everything, and quite frankly, she'd become a wife without him even putting a ring on her yet.

Knock! Knock!

The two knocks on his door made him sigh with frustration. He'd told all his groomsmen that he wanted to be left alone, but they couldn't seem to follow that simple instruction. Reluctantly, he sauntered toward his hotel room door and slowly opened it, only to see his mother on the other side.

"Mama," he greeted her lovingly, opening the door wider for her to step inside.

"Baby, what's wrong?" Her face had a genuine worried look on it as she embraced him into her arms. "You asked all your groomsmen to leave you alone? Why?"

Khaleeq walked back over to the standing mirror he had been in front of. He said nothing and just continued to fiddle with his tie. Seeing him struggle to tie it correctly made Teyana walk over to her son and stand in front of him.

"You never could do it right," she told him with a smirk as she tied it for him. "Khaleeq, baby, talk to me. I can sense something's wrong, so there's no point hiding it from me. I'm your mother, remember?"

Khaleeq sighed, shutting his eyes as he thought about telling his mother about Monalisa. A part of him wanted to keep it all to himself because he didn't want anyone finding out about his affair, but another part of him was desperate to reveal the truth to someone. He had almost revealed the truth to Kisan but failed when they'd been shot at. Honestly, keeping this a secret was starting to drain his soul.

"I'm in love with someone else," he suddenly blurted out as he opened his eyes. "Someone else that isn't April."

Teyana gave him a look of bewilderment, her hands freezing at their action of doing his tie.

"W-What?"

"I'm in love with someone el..." Khaleeq's words suddenly trailed off when his mom brought a finger to his lips, shutting him up.

"I heard you," she whispered in disbelief, lifting her finger off his lips. "I just can't believe it. You told me you loved April and wanted to spend the rest of your life with her. You were so sure on marrying her when I asked you months ago."

"I've fallen for someone else."

"Who?"

"Monalisa."

"Monalisa?" She gave him a wild look. "Monalisa, your wedding planner?"

Khaleeq gave her a guilty nod and sighed once again. He felt like a huge weight had been lifted off his shoulders revealing that to his mother. But as quickly as that weight lifted, it came back once he saw the disappointed look on her face.

"Mom, it was an accident."

"You don't just fall in love with someone else by accident," she said tensely. "Khaleeq, you're supposed to be marrying April. That's the woman you chose, the woman you made a promise to, not Monalisa."

"But Mom, what am I supposed to do? I can't help who I fall in love with! I can't help the way I feel!"

"No you can't," she agreed with him on that one. "But you can make things right. You can still stay loyal to the woman who is currently putting on a wedding dress for you. The woman that has remained loyal to you through it all. You still love April, don't you?"

"I do bu—"

"Then correct your mistake and marry her, Khaleeq," his mother advised. "Marry the woman you're supposed to marry."

"But Mom, how am I supposed to get married to April with Monalisa sitting right there watching?"

"Well," Teyana began quietly, avoiding his direct eye contact. "Monalisa won't be attending today."

"Huh?" The shocked look in his eyes was unmissable. "What do you mean?"

"She called April a few minutes ago to tell her that she's been feeling really ill. So she won't be able to come but wishes you both the best."

Shit. Khaleeq couldn't believe that Monalisa wasn't going to be present today. After all the planning she had put into this wedding, she wasn't even going to be here to witness it. And he loathed that he wasn't going to be able to lay eyes on her, because he really did want to see her.

"So honestly, son, you're not going to have any problems marrying April today."

Khaleeq looked closely at his mother, not really surprised that she wanted him to marry April. She loved April. She'd loved her from the very first moment that Khaleeq had introduced her. Everyone loved April.

Everyone seemed to love April... but the real question was, did he love her enough to marry her today?

CHAPTER 13

~ 24 HOURS LATER ~

"This view is… magnificent," she commented happily. "I can't believe I'm really Mrs. Khaleeq Williams now."

The wedding had happened without a hitch.

Khaleeq had decided to marry April. Monalisa not being present at the wedding had helped quite a lot because he didn't have to see her face in the crowd while he said his vows. Now here they were in the Dominican Republic at their private honeymoon villa. They were here for seven nights only, and he gladly hoped that the seven nights would fly by.

"I'm just glad you didn't get shot somewhere badly. Imagine that," April remarked with horror as she stared at his bandaged shoulder. Finding out that he had gotten shot during their wedding reception was a shock indeed, but he had assured her that he was okay.

Khaleeq examined the bright red bikini that April had on while sitting on the sun bed next to him and instantly felt himself harden in his pants. It did a great job of showing off her figure and cupping her boobs perfectly.

"You happy that we're finally married, honey?" April asked him with a happy smile.

Khaleeq slowly nodded as he kept his eyes sealed on her figure, biting his bottom lip at how attractive she looked.

Noticing the lust growing in his eyes made April only smile harder and get up from her sun-bed. Her husband liked what he could see, and she was about to give him exactly what he wanted.

"Like what you see, Mr. Williams?"

Khaleeq observed as she stood up beside him and her eyes drifted down to the growing tent in the middle of his thighs. Again, he slowly nodded, not bothering to speak up. Because the only thing he truly wanted to see was Monalisa in a red bikini.

April climbed on top of him, sitting comfortably on his lap and wrapping her arms securely around him. Then she branded their lips together and kissed him deeply. The only thing that could keep Khaleeq horny and willing to have sex with his wife right now, were images of a naked Monalisa, laid out on his bed waiting for him.

~ *Two Days Later* ~

"Are we even still together?"

Troy's question made Sabrina look up at him with guilt. She knew why he was questioning her. They rarely saw each other, and when they did see each other, Sabrina was always anxious to leave him claiming she had a lot of work to get done at Solána Rose. The truth was she was anxious to go and be with Kadeem. These days, he seemed really stressed, and she hated to leave his side. Especially when she knew that she could keep his mind clear and keep him at ease.

"I know things have been... distant between us, Troy," Sabrina announced with an honest look as she sat on the couch opposite his.

"Really distant, Sab," Troy added with a frown.

Right now they were at his house due to his demand of seeing her. "Well I've been trying to find the right words to tell you but... I think... I think we should br—"

"Break up?" he interrupted her, finishing off her sentence for her. "You want to break up?"

Sabrina slowly nodded, fear filling her as she looked at the sorrow fill his pupils.

"I think we should."

"That's what you honestly want, Sabrina?" he asked quietly.

"I just feel like it'll be better if we're just fr—"

"You want me to die, Sabrina?"

Hearing him mention his death brought an uneasy feeling to the center of her chest. She was instantly reminded of his suicide attempts.

"'Cause we both know that I can't live without you, Sab," he admitted with teary eyes. "If you leave me again, I don't know what I'll do."

Sabrina could feel the guilt fill her soul again. She didn't want Troy to die because of her. How would she be able to live with herself knowing that she was the cause of his death? It would haunt her forever and ever until she left this earth.

"I don't want you to die, Troy," she pleaded with him. "Please don't say that."

"Then don't leave me," he responded. "Don't leave me and I won't die."

All Sabrina could think about was her conscience. She didn't want to be the cause of Troy's death, and she had a strong gut feeling that if she left him, he would harm himself and potentially end his life.

Things with Kadeem were complicated at this point, but she was sure that they were getting back on track. He was starting to forgive her each day and vice versa with what he had done on her birthday. They had both hurt each other pretty badly, but they were over-coming it.

Now she was stuck in the predicament of being torn between two men; the man that had her heart, and the man that she felt she needed to stay with out of guilt and pity.

LUCIANA LEFT HER FAVORITE BOOK. *You coming to get it?*

Solána.

Kisan had seen her text and instantly smiled. *Thank you, Lu, you've given daddy a way back in,* he mused to himself with delight. And she had because leaving her favorite book during her last visit to Solána meant that Kisan could finally seize the opportunity to have some alone time with Solána. He had dropped Luciana over to Solána's again last weekend because Luciana had begged to see her again. How could he deny his baby girl her wishes?

Only this time he decided to leave his favorite women alone, allowing them to bond without him being present. And seeing the grin on Luciana's face when he had come to pick her up made him smile all day.

Now, here he stood, looking at the woman he loved as she stood in the doorway of her living room with her arms crossed over her chest.

Fuck, why the hell she got on those lil' ass shorts though?

They were black satin shorts that were extremely short and did a great job at clutching her booty. He'd had a nice long view of them when following her into her home, but now that she stood in front of him, he couldn't admire it anymore. But that didn't mean he couldn't admire her cleavage that was peeking under her matching V-neck black crop top.

"Thanks for keeping her shit safe," he thanked Solána with Luciana's favorite book in hand. "I wouldn't have heard the last of it if she'd lost it."

"It's fine," Solána responded with a small smile. "I know how much she loves it."

Kisan gave her a simple head nod before walking toward the exit, which happened to be in the very same direction of where Solána stood.

Solána nervously gazed at him as he sauntered toward her. She absolutely hated how sexy he looked wearing an all-white Nike track-suit. He looked like heaven in the physical. Clean and crisp, with not a single stain or imperfection on his fit.

When she tried to move out of the way for him to pass, he immediately grabbed onto her waist and kept her in place.

"Do you know how much I love you?"

His touch had captivated her instantly. She couldn't even remember the last time she'd felt his hands on her body and now feeling them made her realize how much she'd missed his touch.

"Kisan…"

"Sol, I'm fuckin' tired of this. I'm tired of us not being together."

"You know exactly why we're not together."

"And I've been trying my hardest to make shit work again," he revealed wholeheartedly. "I've been giving you all the mothafuckin' space you need, I've let you meet Luciana… what else do I need to do? Baby, what can I work on as of right now? How can I make you a happier woman? How can I make this relationship between you and I stronger? Just tell a nigga what he needs to do, and I promise you…" He leaned in closer toward her so that their lips were almost touching, and Solána felt herself drowning in his presence. Smelling his seductive cologne was not helping. "I'll do it."

Their eyes remained locked, and Solána could see the love and affection that he had for her. She could see how desperate he was for her to be back in his life how she used to be. As his girlfriend.

"Well for starters," she confidently began. "You need to stop fucking up, Kisan. I told you before, what you did to me was wrong, and I need to be sure that you're never going to do it again."

He gently nodded in response to her words. "A'ight, baby, I got you. I promise."

"I'm not done," she commented, and he gave her a surprised look. "I need to be able to trust you again, Kisan. Trust that you're never going to break my heart again."

Kisan gave her a sincere look while continuing to nod at her, knowing that without a doubt, he would be able to win back her trust.

"That's what you need from a nigga?"

"Yes."

"Consider it done," he promised before branding his lips onto hers, taking her completely by surprise, but nonetheless making her feel happy at the kiss. They hadn't kissed in what felt like forever, so for them to be doing it now, it felt spectacular to the both of them. Like fireworks were shooting off all around them.

As their kiss deepened, Kisan dropped Luciana's book out his hand and grabbed onto both sides of Solána's waist. Then he wrapped his arms around her tighter and pulled her closer to him. Smelling her vanilla scent made his desire for her heighten, and he pulled her as close to him as possible, enabling her to feel the growing bulge in his center.

"S-San... No, we can't," she protested, breaking their lips apart and pulling slightly away from him.

"Why the hell not?" He gave her a strange look before looking down at his pants. "He misses you so damn much."

Solána looked down with him, biting her lips as she stared at how large it had grown underneath his pants. Just staring at it made her want it even more.

"And I know you miss him too."

He was 100 percent right about that. She badly missed and wanted him. But even if they were about to have sex, that didn't mean they were automatically back together, and she made that clear to him before allowing him to kiss her once again.

While they kissed, Kisan lifted her legs and wrapped them around his torso before leading the way to her bedroom. Once arriving, he threw her onto her mattress watching her bounce lightly as he stripped in front of her.

Solána watched with a bated breath as he took each article of clothing off, piece by piece, with his honey brown eyes glued on her. She greatly admired his muscular physique, feeling herself get wet at how good his body looked. It seemed like he had gotten bigger too, because his muscles and abs were looking even more defined.

When he was naked, he pounced on her, noticing how she had been unable to strip because she was too busy watching him get undressed. He knew from the way her eyes lingered on his body that she was loving exactly what she could see. She had clearly missed him.

Gently, he pulled her shorts down her thighs, off her ankles, and chucked them to the side before proceeding to remove her crop top and bra. Once they were off, he lustfully wet his bottom lip as he started sliding her panties down her legs.

Fuck, I've really missed you, girl, he mused as he stared at the wet pearl between her thighs. That pearl that he had missed so greatly, and now more than ever, all he wanted was to taste her.

Solána was immediately taken by surprise at how nasty he got. He didn't even seem to want to take things slow; he just latched his mouth onto her pussy and began to devour her like she was the desert he'd waited his whole life for.

"Oh my," she said with a whimper, watching him suck hungrily on her clit. "Kisan... shit."

Without a doubt she had missed him. She had missed seeing the desire and lust in his eyes that he had only for her. Suddenly, he spat on her, and it only made her excitement grow higher.

Faster and faster, his tongue lapped against her soft bud, rolling his saliva and her juices on her entrance, doing it purposely to drive her crazy. Her sweet juices were already coated over his lips and all over his chin beard, and he absolutely loved it.

"Kisssssan, ssshit," her moans only got louder with each of his maneuvers.

His tongue flicked rapidly against her folds, and Solána felt like she was going to explode with how good it all felt. Kisan was making sweet yet nasty love to her pussy, and she couldn't deny how great it felt. This ecstasy, she had greatly missed. The ecstasy that only he could provide.

"Ughhhh fuck, Kisan!" she continued to moan, feeling her body shake as his tongue suddenly pushed in and out of her tight hole.

"Mm hmm," Kisan groaned against her pussy as he thrusted his tongue in and out of her. "Say my mothafuckin'... name, baby."

"Kisannnn!"

Kisan continued to taste her, his dick growing harder with each drop of her nectar entering his mouth. Everything about her taste, smell, and moans, he loved. He would never be able to stop loving this woman. No matter what. She had his heart forever.

"Kisan... Oh baby..."

When he was finally able to dive deep inside her, Kisan kept his gaze on her as he penetrated her slow and steady.

"I'm sorry, peanut," he apologized with a deep groan. "I'm so sorry I messed up."

His dick pushed all the way inside her, filling her up completely and making her almost want to cry at how good it felt. Too good. If it was possible for her to not ever stop, then she would willingly do it. She just wanted this moment to last forever.

"I love you," he informed her, and all Solána could do was nod at him, unable to speak. She felt like she could feel him in her ribs. That's how deep he was.

"Do you love me?" he queried as he quickly thrusted out of her. Again, all she could do was nod, feeling too high off their sex to speak. But Kisan of course wasn't having that. "Do you?" After his query, the sudden pound of his dick entering back inside her came. "Answer me, Sol," he whispered into her ear, knowing how crazy he was driving her.

"I do, San. Ugh!"

Her hips moved in the fast rhythm that he led. Deeper and faster he fucked her, with his hands gripped onto her waist as he pushed inside her. Their bodies were both burning up by the second, and sweat beads had broken out onto their skin.

"You do?" He grabbed her long legs, pulling them even tighter to his sides so that she couldn't run from his drilling. Every movement she had to feel until it was the only thing she could feel. That was his goal.

"I do!" she declared as his shaft pumped rapidly in her core. "I love you!"

"You love who?" he challenged, wanting her to say exactly what he wanted and how he wanted it.

"You, Kisannnnnn, ahhh!"

Solána felt like her whole entire body was on fire. This pleasure right here that he had started was a dangerous one. He was playing an extremely dangerous game, beating her pussy up and trying to get her to speak up.

"Kisan, who?" he whispered boldly, now licking and sucking her neck.

"Kisannnnnnnn." Her moans only heightened as he started grinding his thick rod between her walls, making her cream quicker all over him.

"Kisan, who?" he repeated, easing in and out of her harder and quicker. "Who the fuck is that?"

"Kisan, ssshit…. Kisan…. Williams!"

"I sure as hell can't fuckin' hear you," he snapped. "And I'm sure your neighbors can't either."

"Kisan mothafuckin' Williams!" she yelled, feeling tears fill her lids. "That's who I love!"

"I know." Kisan grinned cockily before kissing her lips, feeling the pressure rise in his dick.

Solána's bed loudly creaked underneath them, and her headboard was banging against her wall. As their lips remained sealed, that still didn't stop Solána's whimpers and moans. She could feel her pressure quickly building between her thighs, and her hands quickly clutched his back, scratching and clawing away at it with her nails as her climax approached.

"Shit… I swear on everything," Kisan announced as he broke their kiss. "If you ever give my pussy away, I'll kill him and you, Sol."

The sounds of his dick fucking her, his ball sac hitting her entrance, and both their moans sounded louder. Solána's hips rocked faster and faster against his. Any minute now, she was about to cum.

"You gon' cum for me or what?" Kisan taunted her, gripping onto her waist tighter.

"Yasssss," she replied passionately, her eyes rolling back. "Kisan… shit, I'm gonna cu… uhh!" Her loud gasp sounded, and her breathing heightened. She reached for his neck, choking him in the hopes that it would help ease the intense euphoria coming in.

"Ughhhh!" Her fingertips pressed firmly into his neck, holding him tighter, as she pumped her hips up and down. Her body began to tense in his arms. "Kisan!" she cried out as her body froze underneath him. Her release went straight to the top of his shaft, covering every inch.

"Aghh shit, Sol," he groaned one last time, giving one last hard thrust before his climax shot inside her warm cave. "I fuckin' love you... so damn much, girl."

CHAPTER 14

"What's up, Mr. Married," Kisan friendly greeted his younger cousin over the phone. He had been thinking about Khaleeq a lot since his wedding, and right now was the perfect time to check up on him. "How's the honeymoon going?"

"Alright," Khaleeq mumbled. "I'm just ready to get back home."

"To Monalisa?"

Khaleeq's heart began to race. "Nigga, how did you know? I never finished telling you who it was."

"You ain't have to," Kisan responded knowingly. "I know she's been around because she was planning the wedding, and not seeing her at the wedding made it all make sense. You've been fuckin' your wedding planner this whole entire time, Leeq?"

Khaleeq sighed deeply before answering, "Shit started off as an accident. We both had way too much to drink one night I was looking for April, and we just got carried away. You know what a can of Four Loko can do, nigga. I told myself that it was a one-time thing. I was never going back there again, but then she came 'round the house looking too fuckin' sexy, and I just had to… I just had to get a taste of her again."

"Nigga, you ain't been able to stop having a taste of her," Kisan told him tensely. "You said you love her, but are you sure you love her or the pleasure she brings?"

"I tried to convince myself it was just lust too," Khaleeq revealed. "But it's not. I'm in love with her."

"Which makes no damn sense 'cause you just got married to April. What you gonna do then, divorce her?"

"I don't even know," Khaleeq whispered with regret. "This shit is messed all the way up... I'ma need you to promise me one thing though, Mace."

"What's that?" Kisan queried with curiosity.

"Don't tell Solána," Khaleeq requested. "I know you guys are getting back on track and shit, but I know Monalisa didn't want anyone to know about us. She didn't even tell her sisters... well her cousins. You heard about that foul shit their aunt did, right?"

"Oh yeah, Solána told me," Kisan said with a pout, thinking about what Carolina had kept secret from the girls for so long. "That shit was terrible... But yeah, you've got my word. I won't tell her."

"Thank you."

"Well I gotta go right now, nigga. I've got a date with Sol in a few, but I'ma see you soon, right? You coming back in a few days?"

"Yeah, yeah two more days, and I'm back."

"A'ight. Holla at you later then."

"For sure."

Kisan ended the call and left his phone on his velvet ottoman before getting ready for the date he had planned for Solána tonight. He was about to do something completely out of his comfort zone, but he was more than willing to do it for her.

Hours later, Solána had arrived at his crib and was welcomed to Kisan in a robe, which she found odd, until he led her to his dining room and took it off.

"Oh wow... Kisan... I don't believe this right now..." A light giggle escaped her lips. Kisan had prepared a three-course meal for her. He had laid out a single table with a red tablecloth, red rose petals on the floor around the table, and scented lavender candles. She loved the romantic vibe he had set up for her, but she especially loved what he was wearing.

"Told you I was gonna make shit up to you," he reminded her with a sexy smirk as he pulled out her chair and watched her take her seat. "I can't believe I'm doing this shit either. You got me wearing this tight ass shit... Fuck it though. Anything for you, baby. You know that."

Solána's smile couldn't stop growing as she watched him. He wasn't wearing any clothes except for the burgundy bow tie around his neck and matching lace boxers.

"You went into a store to buy that, right?" she asked, staring at his lace boxers and smiling wider.

"Hell fuckin' nah," he snapped with a frown. "I got my assistant at the car company to go get this shit for me. What the fuck a gangsta like me doing in a sex shop?"

"I'm taking you one day." Solána laughed as she watched him reach for the champagne bottle on the table. "You're gonna love it."

"I doubt that shit very much," he responded as he poured some champagne into her wine glass only to suddenly stop when he felt her hand start stroking his thigh. "Sol..."

"I just wanted to feel the material," she lustfully remarked, eyeing it closely but more so looking at his bulge. "It's so nice and soft." Her hands moved from his thigh to the center of his boxers so that she could stroke his growing manhood.

"Uh-uh." Kisan stepped away from her so that she could no longer stroke him through his boxers. "Not yet, baby. Daddy's gotta serve you first. I'ma give what you want later, I promise. It's gon' be your dessert."

She shyly looked up at him before nodding and letting him proceed in pouring her some more champagne. One thing was for certain: she couldn't wait to get to dessert.

I'MA NEED you niggas to back the fuck off or shit won't be nice at all.
Send.

Kadeem had never felt more on edge as he did now.

It didn't help that Kisan and his father, Axel, was determined to find out who had shot Khaleeq, but knowing who was behind the shooting definitely didn't help Kadeem's conscience.

The Serbians were not backing off, and to make matters even worse, they didn't even want to meet up with him to talk about things. They were adamant on knocking The Williams off their mighty horse, one by one, even if that included Kadeem himself.

All Kadeem could feel was regret. Regret for being greedy and trying to take the crown from his uncles and his father. A crown that he had been born into, and a crown that he'd always had to share.

What the fuck had gotten into me? It had to be the day he saw Sabrina cheat on him with Troy. That's when he had cooked up the wild idea of wanting to do things his way in the first place. But now looking back, he realized how selfish and stupid he had been.

He lived a really good life with his cousins and his father. A really good life being at the top together. Why he would ever want to ruin that, he did not know.

"Would you like me to make you something to eat, love?"

Kadeem looked up from his bright screen only to see Sabrina walking into his bedroom with a large smile. She looked so pretty, and having her around his crib made him feel with peace and slight happiness. He wasn't completely happy because he knew that she didn't belong to him like she used to.

Yeah, she had cheated on him, and yeah, he had gotten his revenge by making her watch him fuck another girl, but Kadeem was quickly getting over it. At this point, all he wanted was for them to be back together and to move on with their relationship.

He shook his head 'no' in response to her question before deciding to speak up. "But I'ma tell you what I do want though."

"What's that, babe?" She came to stand in front of him before straddling him and wrapping her arms around his neck.

"I need you," he began, moving his hand across her back and down till he was able to squeeze her ass, "to leave that clown ass nigga for good."

Sabrina froze with fear at his request, not sure what to say in response. How could she leave Troy at a time like this? A time where he was vulnerable and bound to harm himself without her being his girlfriend.

"Dee, you know I can't le—"

"I'm not asking you, Sabrina. I'm telling you," he snapped. "You either leave him or I kill him, so you'll have no choice but to leave him either way."

"You can't kill hi... Kadeem, he could kill himself without me," she explained gently, staring deeply into his pupils. "Please don't make me do this."

"Sabrina, why can't you see that he's manipulating you to stay with him?" he questioned her firmly. "If that nigga really wanted to kill himself, he would have been done it. And hey, if he does, then cool. That means I don't have to do it."

Sabrina gave him a look of horror and disbelief, but he ignored it and pecked her lips before lifting her off his lap. He placed her on his bed and got up, ready to go hop in the shower.

"I don't mind what you make me, as long as I get to have that pussy for desert," he commented with a smirk before lifting his shirt off his body.

Sabrina watched as he undressed in front of her, still in disbelief at what he wanted her to do. Breaking up with Troy was something that she had already tried and failed to complete. So how on earth was she supposed to do it now?

MONALISA COULDN'T BELIEVE she was back here. Honestly, she didn't want to be back here, but her Aunt... *her mother,* had begged to see her. So she decided to give her a chance and see what she wanted.

"I just want us to be able to mend our relationship and work on getting back to how we used to be," Carolina explained wholeheartedly, gazing at her daughter and hoping that she would be willing to move on from this situation. "I am so sorry at what I did to you,

Mona. I'm sorry that I ruined the trust you had for me. I'm so sorry."

Monalisa took a glance at her phone that sat on the kitchen table she was seated at. No notifications had come in, but looking at her phone was what she'd rather do than look at her mother. Because the more she stared at Carolina, the more she wanted to cry.

To know that her mother had not only abandoned her when she was younger but continued to play along like she was her auntie when in reality she was not, truly hurt. The hurt she felt was a hurt she had never felt before.

Unable to stop them, Mona's tears came falling out of her eyes, and she sighed in defeat at the fact that Carolina had gotten her so emotional over this situation again. This situation that she wished had never happened in the first place.

"I just can't believe... I just can't believe you lied to me." She sobbed, feeling a sharp pain in the center of her chest. The sharp pain was the heartbreak she could constantly feel. "Fair enough you left, but you should have just been straight up about it and told me who you really were. I've lived with the lie of thinking that my mother has been dead, when in reality she's sitting right in front of me."

Carolina's tears also dropped out of her lids as she watched her daughter sob. She felt so ashamed knowing that she had done this to her. Knowing that she had broken her heart. Knowing that she had put her in this terrible situation.

"Mona, love... I'm so sorry. If I could take it all back and start over, I swear I would. I would start over and be a much better mother to you. But I want to make things right. I know how bad this situation is, but please, Mona, just let me make the effort to make things right."

Monalisa listened to her mother's words and remained silent. Deep down she knew she was going to have to allow her mother to make things right between them. There was no way that she was going to permanently kick her out of her life. How could she when Carolina was her mother? Her real mother.

It would take some time, but Mona needed to learn how to forgive her mother for the crime she had committed.

CHAPTER 15

~ 1 MONTH LATER ~

Oh my Lord, what does this girl want now?
Dazhanae thought that she had gotten April out of her life for good. But from the missed calls and left voicemails on her phone, she had thought wrong.

"Dazhanae. It's April. Don't know if you deleted my number or not, but we need to talk. Please hit me up as soon as you get this."

"Hello, Dazhanae. It's April. Again. Not sure why you keep on missing my calls, but we really do need to talk. Please call me back ASAP. Don't ignore this."

All Dazhanae did was send all of April's voicemails to the trash and decided to forget about them. April had gotten the DNA test she needed, so what else did she want from her? Right now, anyway, Dazhanae had something else heavy on her mind. Luciana wasn't home, and neither was Kisan. And she hoped to God that this nigga hadn't taken her to go see the bitch he claimed to love.

Kisan, where is Luciana?

Dazhanae.

Seeing Dazhanae's text message appear on his screen made Kisan roll his eyes with annoyance before locking off his phone and concentrating back on Solána and Luciana. Luciana was currently getting her hair braided by Solána, and the act of them talking together while she braided Luciana's hair truly warmed Kisan's heart.

They had gotten to know each other so well and were bonding like two best friends who never wanted to leave each other's side. He loved seeing how close they had become. The two girls that he loved, getting along just how he wanted them to.

Kisan!!!! Where is my daughter?

Dazhanae.

Kisan: *Relax with the exclamation points before I come over to where you at and prove a real point by choking you the fuck out.*

Dazhanae: *Where is my baby?*

Kisan: *She's fine. With her father.*

Kisan: *Now shut the fuck up.*

After his last text message, Kisan's phone stopped lighting up with text messages from Dazhanae, and he could focus on his girls bonding in peace.

∼

ANOTHER DAY, another dollar.

Monalisa was glad to hear that April had gotten married to her man without a hitch. At this point, Monalisa just wanted to move on with her life and forget all about him. And she was doing just that.

Right now, she was standing up in front of her desk and looking over the details for her new client who was getting married at the end of the year. They wanted a small and intimate wedding, so this wasn't going to be a challenge for Monalisa at all. She was glad to finally be able to plan a smaller wedding in comparison to April's extravagant wedding that she didn't even attend. But she had seen the pictures that April had sent over, and it truly looked magnificent.

"So they want a beach wedding... Cute. I can definitely do that," Monalisa said to herself. Talking to herself was something that she always did when it came to planning weddings. She liked to be able to talk things out and see where her mind was at with things.

Knock! Knock!

"Monalisa, there's—"

Without looking up from her desk, Monalisa dismissed her assistant. "Nope, nope, Angela, I'm in the middle of something right now. Whatever it is or whoever it is can wait."

"I can't wait," his deep voice sounded through her office, making her head instantly pop up. "I'm done waiting."

Oh God. Monalisa hated how good he looked right now. He was dressed casual in gray Nike sweats, a white t-shirt, and matching white Nike Air Force 1's on his feet. A casual fit, but he still managed to make it look so damn sexy.

Angela, her assistant, sensed the instant tension growing in the room and decided to take her departure, shutting Monalisa's office door behind her.

"Get out," Monalisa ordered firmly, looking back at the notes on her white oak desk.

"Mona."

"Get out. Get out. Get out," she quickly repeated, feeling her breaths quicken. "You're married now. I can't have anything to do with you."

"Mona."

"Get out," she said once again, looking up to see him still standing by her office door. "Leave me alone."

"Now we both know there's no way I can do that shit," he told her seriously before walking toward her desk. "Mona, I can't stay away from you when you're all I think about 24/7."

"You need to be thinking about April 24/7. Not me. Khaleeq, plea… what are you doing?" she asked, seeing that he hadn't stopped in front of her desk and was now walking around her desk. "Khaleeq, stop. Stay away." She stepped back, seeing that he was now walking straight toward her. "Khaleeq, no. Don't come any closer."

"Why?" he queried, wanting to know her reasons behind not wanting him to be near her. "Why you scared of a nigga all of a sudden? You know I've already touched every single part of your gorgeous body."

"Khaleeq," she called out to him once more, taking a few steps back until she was at the far edge of her desk. Khaleeq ignored her and still made his way closer to her. Just when she was about to turn away, he grabbed her arm and pulled her into his arms.

"Khaleeq, please... go," she whispered nervously, now smelling his alluring scent and getting high off it. Feeling those hands on her body was making her heat up with desire for him. *Fuck, I've missed him.*

"Go where?" he genuinely asked, looking down at her carefully. "Where the fuck am I gonna go unless it's to you?"

"You're married, Khaleeq," she reminded him, plucking up the courage to finally look him in the eyes. She quickly regretted it, because those brown eyes were looking at her with the most love and affection. "Married to Ap—"

"Fuck her," he fumed. "I'm leaving her."

"No you ain't," Monalisa disagreed. "You just married her."

"And I'm just gonna divorce her," he coolly stated. "Watch me."

"No, Khaleeq," she protested, trying to push him away. "I'm not gonna be responsible for your marriage failing!"

"Monalisa, I never wanted to marry her in the first place!" he exclaimed with a deep exhale. "The fact that I was never interested in planning the wedding showed that to me. I was just too blind to see it. But then you came along... you came along and opened up everything clearly for me. I'm leaving her, and whether you want to be with a nigga or not, it's happening. I don't love her enough to spend the rest of my life with her, and that's that. Nothing's gonna change that shit."

Monalisa gave him a shocked look before looking away from him. Suddenly, she felt her chin being pulled back in his direction, and her eyes were back on his.

"I love you, Monalisa Claudette Winters," he announced lovingly. "Ain't nobody gon' be able to change that." Then he pressed their lips together so that he could give her a kiss.

Monalisa could feel butterflies flying in her stomach. This was the first time he had told her that he loved her, and now that she was hearing it, she didn't want to stop hearing it. Quite frankly, she loved him too, and she wanted him to know that, so she pulled their lips apart.

"I love you too, Khaleeq Clarence Williams."

Both of them declaring their love for one another was the matchstick to set fire to their libidos. Their lips instantly sealed back together, and as his tongue slipped into her mouth, Khaleeq pulled her toward her desk about to place her on top when he noticed the stuff she had on the top. He cleared her desk with his hands, sending her papers to the floor before sitting her on top.

Monalisa had her eyes shut while they kissed, but that didn't stop her hands from finding their way to his sweats and instantly pulling them down. Once his sweats were down, Khaleeq feeling grateful that she was wearing a skirt today, lifted it up and snatched down her thong.

He positioned himself between her legs and secured them around his torso before diving right in. He guided his thickness through her passage and slowly filled her up. His hands were gripped onto her waist, allowing him to ease himself deeper between her folds.

"Oh my... Khaleeq," she moaned as his shaft rested deep into her pussy.

She kept her legs in place around his torso and had her arms around his neck and began rocking her body with his thrusts that seemed to be getting quicker with each passing second.

By now, their lips had separated, enabling them to stare at each other, and through both their eyes, they could see the burning passion they had for each other. This was all they had wanted for the past two weeks away from each other. This was all they needed, to just be together.

"I fuckin' missed you, baby," he groaned, pecking her soft lips and repeatedly thrusted his hips forward into her.

"I missed you more," Mona whimpered loudly as Khaleeq pushed faster and deeper into her tightness.

"Fuck!" He buried himself more and more into her, wanting to make sure she felt him in her guts. "You ain't given my shit away to no nigga, right?"

She shook her head 'no' at him, her head feeling dizzy with lust as he continued to pump into her.

"You ain't?"

"Nooo," she cried.

"You sure?"

"I ain't! I promise!" she moaned louder, realizing that her assistant could probably hear her right now, but she didn't care.

"This my shit," he announced proudly as he lifted his hand to her throat and choked her. "Mine only. No one else's. Right, Mona?" he asked her as he thrust his shaft hard into her.

"Ahhh, right. Yours."

"Khaleeq's pussy?"

"Khaleeq's pussy, baby," she passionately repeated after him.

"I'm marrying you... I'm marrying this pussy. You're mine forever, Mona."

"Yes, baby. Forever yours."

Khaleeq's groans sounded louder as he continued to pound inside her. He had missed this. He had missed feeling this pleasure with her, and he had most definitely missed beating her pussy up.

"Open your mouth," Khaleeq aggressively demanded, making Monalisa smile as she did as he wanted. She opened her mouth for him, and before she knew it he spat into it. It was a weird act, but nonetheless, it turned her all the way on, because at this point, her desire for this man had completely shot through the roof. She wanted him more than ever, so being able to taste him was intoxicating. Khaleeq then branded their lips together in a loving kiss and continued to ride her.

All he knew was that he was never letting her go, and leaving April was a must.

SABRINA TOOK a deep breath before opening her front door only to be greeted by Troy's handsome face. Kadeem had let her not say a word to Troy about breaking up for a whole month. But today, her time was officially up. Kadeem wanted her to end things with him so that they could focus on them again without Troy being in the picture.

"Sab."

"Hi," she plainly said, opening the door as wide as it could go. "Come on in."

"Is this something serious?" he asked, stepping in. "Your text sounded serious."

"It is," she admitted, watching him closely. "We need to talk."

"What about?"

"Have a seat and I'll let you know," she explained calmly, and Troy did as she asked, walking deeper into her living room and taking a seat on her couch. Sabrina then followed and took the empty seat next to him.

She'd had a few days to prepare herself for what she was about to say, so she wasn't worried on how to say it. She was more worried about how he would react and how he would try to get her to change her mind, but Sabrina was sure on her decision. She wanted to move on with her relationship with Kadeem.

"Troy, I'm breaking up with you," she confidently announced. "And I know what you're about to say, but I'm going to have to ask you not to say it. You're a grown ass man, Troy, and you don't need me to keep you alive. This relationship was a mistake; having sex with you was a big mistake, especially since I was in the best relationship that I had been in for a long time. I just think it's best if you and I break up. I want to move on from you and fix things with my new relationship. I'm hoping that you can accept this and be happy for me. Move on and find love with someone else."

After her words, Sabrina let out the long breath that she had been holding and kept both eyes glued on Troy's. She couldn't read the look on his face because it was a confusing one. She couldn't tell if he was sad, angry, or calm.

"...Troy? Did you hear me?" she asked gently. "I said I'm breaking up with yo—"

Wham!

Sabrina thought that she had been dreaming. She thought that she had been dreaming when she felt the hard hit of his hand against her cheek. But once she realized that she had been thrown back against her seat and her hand was on her burning skin, she knew that he had hit her.

"Troy! Why the hel—"

Wham! Wham! Wham!

More of his hits followed, and Sabrina tried her hardest to push him away. But he was no match for her. He was stronger and more amped up in giving her assaults.

Wham! Wham! Wham!

She'd tried to block his hits, but they just kept coming. One by one, harder and harder, punches came landing on her face, all over her body. Her screams and shouts filled her apartment, but it was no use.

"You stupid, selfish little bitch! You really think I'm letting you go?"

Wham! Wham! Wham!

No one was coming to save her from this monster.

CHAPTER 16

ina, you okay? Just texting to see how you are. Haven't heard from you for a few days now.
Solána.

Ri. Why aren't you picking up any of our calls? Are you okay?
Monalisa.

Sabrina hadn't left the house in two days. She hadn't returned any of her sisters' calls, and she most definitely hadn't returned any of their texts. She hadn't been able to move out her bed because, firstly, she didn't have the strength to, and secondly, she just didn't want to. The only times she got out of bed was to use the bathroom, and even then, she made sure all the lights were off so that she couldn't see herself in the mirror.

However, she knew that if she didn't try to shower and eat something, she could potentially make her health worse than it already was. So Sabrina finally plucked up the courage to get out of bed and head to the shower, only to catch a glimpse of her face in the mirror as she turned the lights on.

Oh God.

She never knew her face could look as horrible as it looked now.

Troy had completely battered her face. She had two swollen, puffy red eyes, a swollen lip, and painful scratches on her face.

Avoiding the mirror had been something she had done for so long because she didn't want to have to face the reality of what had been done to her. However, now she had no choice but to look at her face, and seeing it only made her burst into tears. Everywhere hurt, including her face. Her arms hurt, her legs hurt, her chest hurt... everywhere. Everywhere that he had assaulted her badly ached.

Why hadn't she gone to police?

Sabrina didn't even know. She was still in shock at what Troy had done to her because he had never laid his hands on her before. He had never hurt her in this horrific way before, so for him to do it now, Sabrina was full of horror and surprise.

Sabrina, you can't stay locked up in here in silence. You need to tell someone what he did. Hiding just wasn't going to cut it anymore, and Sabrina knew that, but truth be told, she was afraid of having to face everyone when she looked like this.

> *You only show me love*
> *When it comes to the music*
> *It's like when I feel lonely*
> *That's when you start actin' choosey*

Hearing her phone ring in the distance made her instantly turn to the bathroom door. No one knew what had happened to her because she was too afraid and ashamed to tell anyone about it. The one thing she had promised herself in this life was to never let a man put his hands on her. But she had been too weak and defenseless to fight Troy off.

> *I don't wanna keep playin' them games*
> *'Cause I feel like I'm losin'*
> *I don't wanna keep playin' them games*
> *'Cause I feel like I'm losin'*

No, enough of this weak shit. I need to let them all know. Now. She had ignored the calls from her sisters and Kadeem for far too long. It was time to reveal to everyone what had happened to her. Sabrina quickly left the bathroom, hoping to catch whoever was calling her before her phone locked off, and fortunately, she did.

"Sabrina, honey."

It was Auntie Carolina. And even though she hadn't talked to her in what felt like forever, Sabrina was extremely glad and thankful to hear her soft voice now. Now more than ever, she needed her mother figure to come to her rescue.

"A-Auntie."

Carolina could hear the pain in Sabrina's voice, and it made her instantly get out of her seat. Then she began looking for her shoes and her bag, knowing that she was leaving her home right now to head to Sabrina.

"I'm on my way, baby."

~

"MM, FEELS GOOD..."

Solána smiled to herself as she laid on her chest while his hands massaged her smooth upper back.

"Just good?" Kisan asked as he gently rubbed his hands toward her lower back before reaching the crack of her butt. His hands were currently drenched in the jojoba oil that he had smeared all over his hands and now her entire back.

"Really good, San," she moaned as his palms started stroking her ass. She hadn't even realized how bad she'd needed a massage. Her entire body had been tensed these past few months from working Solána Rose and the drama in her life. But her man had come to her rescue and provided her with the relief that she needed. Feeling his large hands all over her body was everything to her right now.

"Fuck, a nigga got the best view right now," he sexually remarked as he kept on rubbing her butt and took a peek between her thighs at her pussy. "You wet for me right now, Sol?"

"Mm hmm," she moaned, too high off the pleasure that his hands were giving her to really reply. But when she felt his finger slide onto her pearl, she spoke up. "San..."

"You wet for me," he said with a smile, beginning to gently play with her wet bud with a single finger. "So fuckin' wet for me..."

"Mm, Kisan..."

"I wanna play with my pussy real quick," he explained lustfully. "You gon' let me play with her, Solána?"

"Mm hmm," she continued to gently moan as she felt one finger enter her, followed by his second one. Then he started pushing in and out of her, and the pleasure quickly came rushing through her body. "Ahhh, Kisan."

"Relax baby. You know I got yo—"

I just turned, just turned down your avenue
I had to but I'm mad at you

Solána's phone was lying directly in front of her because she had been checking her emails before Kisan had decided to give her a massage, so she could see exactly who was trying to get in touch with her right now during this intimate moment with Kisan.

"Ignore it, Sol."

As much as she wanted to, there was a gut feeling inside her telling her that she needed to answer her phone. And seeing that it was her auntie calling her only enticed her to want to answer the call. But the pleasure that Kisan was providing right now was enough to make her ignore it after all.

I just turned, just turned down your avenue
I had to but I'm mad at you

Ignoring it was her plan until Monalisa's name appeared as the caller ID. That's when she knew something serious was going on.

"Baby, I need to answer this," she informed Kisan, which resulted in him reluctantly pulling his fingers out of her and move slightly away from her. While she answered her phone, Kisan placed his fingers into his mouth, sucking off her juices. Solána turned around to lay on her back and looked up at Kisan. Seeing him suck his fingers turned her on greatly, but when Monalisa started talking, her attention diverted away from him.

"Mona... Sorry, I was busy... What's up?... What do you mean you can't say over the phone?... Where?... Okay. I'm on my way."

Monalisa's phone call had been extremely vague. But now that Solána had arrived at Auntie Carolina's home and laid eyes on Sabrina, she didn't need an explanation. Sabrina's face said it all.

"I'm going to kill him myself!" Solána yelled furiously. "I'm actually going to kill him! How could he do this?"

"Solána, please, calm down," Carolina pleaded with her niece.

"Calm do..." Solána took a deep breath before speaking up again. "Calm down? How can I calm down when my sister's face looks like that?"

Solána felt disgusted. Disgusted at how badly bruised and battered her sister's face was. She had been beaten like an animal, and Solána more than ever wanted Troy in a coffin.

"We need to call the cops! Why you haven't done so already, I don't understand!"

"She said she doesn't want the police involved," Monalisa voiced sadly.

"Sabrina, he needs to pay for what he's done! You can't let him get away with this shit," Solána fumed. "He could have killed you all because you no longer want to be with him. He's not getting away with this! I won't allow it. If you don't want to call the cops, then let's at least tell Kad—"

"No," Sabrina finally spoke up. "Kadeem can't find out. Neither can Kisan. Solána, you know what they'll do to him."

The Winters were all aware of the heavy clout that The Williams had in the streets. They each knew the men that they loved and what they were capable of. How could they not know?

"He deserves it!" Solána protested. "He deserves it all! Sabrina..." Solána walked over to where Sabrina sat on the couch and crouched down in front of her. "No man should ever put his hands on a woman. No man should ever make a woman look like this."

As she kept both eyes on Sabrina, Solána wanted to cry. She wanted to cry because of how horrible this situation was. Her beautiful sister had been hurt in the worst way possible. Abused.

"Don't tell them, Solána," Sabrina affirmed with teary eyes. "Please don't."

~

DON'T you just hate it when people keep on bugging you? Well that's exactly how Dazhanae felt at this moment in time, and she wanted to get April off her back. Today.

"Why do you keep on hitting me up, April? I told you our friendship is over," Dazhanae fumed while crossing her arms across her chest.

April had requested to meet her outside her house, and now they were in April's Mercedes. This was the last place that Dazhanae wanted to be at right now. But with the way April kept on harassing her with calls and texts, without explaining what exactly it was that she wanted, Dazhanae had no choice but to meet up with her.

"I'm not hitting you up about our friendship," April explained in a nonchalant tone which brought a scowl onto Dazhanae's face as she watched her.

"So why do you keep on hitting me up?" Dazhanae asked. "I've already proved to you that Kisan is the father of my child, so what more do you want from me? You're really starting to get on my very last nerve. You think marriage would have kept you busy, but here you are, still meddling in my life."

"You're starting to get on my very last nerve, Dazhanae," April stated rudely, using her words against her. "You wanna know the reason I've been hitting you up?"

"Please enlighten me," Dazhanae said in a fake excited tone.

"I've been hitting you up because I found out your dirty little secret."

Dazhanae gave her a confused look. "What dirty little secret?"

"I know you faked the DNA results, Dazhanae."

Dazhanae appeared to be unfazed by April's revelation and stayed looking at her with a confused facial expression.

"I have no idea what you're talking about, Ap—"

"Oh, cut the bullshit, Dazhanae," April snapped. "I know you faked the DNA results because I got a detective to look into them for me." Dazhanae's heart began to speed up with fear. "You really thought that you could hand me a piece of paper and I wouldn't get them double checked?"

Her heart began to speed up faster and faster as she kept both eyes sealed on April. Knowing that April knew that she had faked the DNA results had officially made her life a living hell.

"You have two days to tell Kisan that he's not the father of Luciana," April threatened her lightly. "Or I'm not only going to tell Khaleeq, I'm going to tell Kisan myself."

"April, you can—"

"Two days is a perfect amount of time for you to prepare yourself on how to tell Kisan, because we both know how he is, and you're going to need time to figure out how you're going to tell him without him killing you. And since you faked the DNA results, I know how sneaky you are, and I know you'll try anything to not let this truth come out. In case you didn't notice, I've got two security cars following me around town since Khaleeq's shooting plus security constantly patrolling my house. Which means that you trying any more funny business won't work, Dazhanae. I have Kisan's number on speed dial, so if I find out you haven't done it, I will call him and let him know. You're not getting out of this shit no more, bitch. I won't let you. Now get the fuck out of my car."

CHAPTER 17

"*M*o..." His kisses landed on her forehead. "Tell me..." Her cheeks. "What's wrong?" Her lips. All over her face wherever he could plant kisses, he did. He had sensed her depressed mood from the second he laid eyes on her, and now more than ever, he wanted to fix it. But in order to do that, he needed to know what was wrong.

Monalisa didn't know if telling Khaleeq was the right thing to do. She anxiously wanted to tell him, but she remembered Sabrina saying how she didn't want Kadeem or Kisan to know. And telling Khaleeq would mean that they would find out within the next few hours. Minutes even.

Monalisa was still traumatized by what Troy had done to Sabrina. Despite everything, Sabrina was still her baby sister, and all she ever wanted to do in this life was protect her sisters. To know that someone as evil as Troy had abused her in the worst way made Monalisa wish death on him. She'd never wished death on anyone before, so this was definitely a first.

"Baby," Khaleeq firmly called out to her. But when she remained silent and didn't say anything, he lifted her chin up and made her look up into his eyes. "Tell me what's wrong. Right now."

THE PUREST LOVE FOR THE COLDEST THUG 2

Monalisa swallowed hard as she gazed up at him. The only thing that was stopping her from blurting out what had happened to Sabrina was Sabrina. Getting The Williams involved would only mean one thing for Troy: *death*. And Sabrina would definitely question both her sisters on how The Williams had found out in the first place. Solána would swear that she never told Kisan, and that would leave Monalisa having to reveal that she had told Khaleeq, thus revealing her situation with Khaleeq.

"It's not a request, Mo," he pushed. "Tell me."

So Monalisa told him. She told him what Troy had done to Sabrina, and she watched the way his jaw started twitching. The vein in his forehead popped out, and a vicious look formed in his eyes.

"Khaleeq, you can't tell Kad—"

"The fuck I'm not," he retorted, leaving her side and rolling off her bed. Anger had completely clouded his thoughts, and more than ever, all he wanted to do was attack someone. Troy in particular.

"Leeq! You can't! Please..." she begged, observing as he started pacing back and forth in front of her bed, his fists tightly clenched by his sides. "I wasn't even supposed to tell you."

"And I'm glad you did!" he shouted. "No way I'm 'bout to let this shit fly! And Kadeem sure as hell won't!"

"Khaleeq, please..."

"Only a bitch ass nigga puts his hands on a woman! But it's cool; he's a *dead* bitch ass nigga."

Monalisa's heart began to speed with panic, and her body temperature began to heat up.

I should have just kept my mouth shut, she mused, regret filling her because of her decision to tell Khaleeq. She lowkey hated how persuasive he was with those sexy eyes of his and that commanding voice. All he had to say were a few words, and she would do whatever he wanted.

Sensing Mona's panic, Khaleeq decided to stop pacing and climb back onto the bed to be back next to her. Once near, he slid himself back in the position he had been with her in his arms and kept her close.

"I promise you, Mona," he gently announced as he pecked her forehead. "He's going to pay for what he's done."

"But Sabrina didn't want you guys involved... She just..."

"She just what? Wants him to get away with the bullshit he did to her?" he asked her incredulously. "Kadeem won't let that shit happen, and whether you told me or not, he was bound to find out."

Monalisa sighed deeply as she snuggled closer against his chest.

"Please don't tell him straight away... Let me at least tell Sabrina that I told you. Maybe she'll end up telling him herself."

"A'ight," he calmly responded. "But I'm telling him by the end of today, Mo, so you need to tell her ASAP. You sure about telling Sabrina though? 'Cause if you do that, then that means you're going to have to tell Sabrina why you're even talking to me in the first place and reveal that you and I ar—"

"Are fucking," she finished off his words for him. "I know."

"Are together," he corrected her, reaching for her hand and holding it in his. "You ready for everyone to know?"

She nodded confidently, and it brought a smile to his lips.

"Good," he happily stated. "'Cause I'm leaving April today."

Monalisa turned to look at him, giving him a shocked look.

"You are?"

"Yup," he confirmed with a sure nod. "I'm sick of playing these games. You're who I want to be with, so I'm making that shit a reality today, officially."

Monalisa gave him a loving smile before leaning in toward his lips and kissing him deeply.

Four hours later, Khaleeq had left Monalisa which meant that it was time for her to give her cousins a call and tell them the truth about what she had been doing behind their backs for the past few months.

"Mona?"

"Ri," Monalisa gently called out to Sabrina, happy to hear her voice. "Solána, you there?"

"Here," Solána voiced. "What's up? You said you wanted to do a three-way call?"

"Yeah, I did," Monalisa said with a light sigh. "There's something I've been needing to tell you guys for the longest, and I know I need to tell you guys right now."

"What is it?" Sabrina asked in a worried tone, thinking that something bad had happened. "You're not hurt, are you?"

"No, no," Monalisa dismissed her worry. "I... I've been sleeping with Khaleeq."

A long pause came after Monalisa's revelation before Solána suddenly spoke up.

"Wait, wait, wait a minute... Khaleeq Williams? As in Kisan's cousin, Khaleeq?"

Sabrina let out a loud gasp. "Married Khaleeq?"

"Yes," Monalisa mumbled. "Khaleeq Williams."

"Oh my God," Sabrina voiced. "Oh my God. Oh my God. Oh my God."

"Please, Ri, calm down."

"You've been sleeping with Khaleeq?" Solána asked again. "For how long? How did this even happen? You don't even know each oth... Oh." Solána finally remembered that Monalisa had been his wedding planner. "Ohhhhhhh shit. Of course, it all makes sense now. You were planning his wedding... you were always around... oh, Mona."

"It was an accident."

"You've been getting dicked down by a Williams and didn't even feel to tell us? Me at least?" Sabrina queried. "And what do you mean it was an accident? His dick didn't just accidentally fall inside you, sis."

"He married April though. So unless you guys have stopped fooling around... oh, you haven't, have you? That's why you're telling us now."

"Yeah, we're still messing around," Monalisa admitted. "I didn't know how to tell you both, especially with his situation, but he's decided that he's leaving April."

"He's leaving April? They just got married like five seconds ago," Sabrina stated with disapproval.

"We love each other."

"Whoa, love? Are you sure about that?" Solána couldn't believe the words coming out from Monalisa's mouth.

"Yes, Sol. We love each other, and we're going to be together. He's the first man that I can honestly say I adore, and I really do want to see where this goes... I know this shit is complicated, but he's determined to make things right. So, he's leaving April today."

"Today, bitch?" Sabrina's shock couldn't be hidden. "Damn, you have him sprung indeed. Most married niggas never leave their wives."

"And he noticed how upset I was about you, Sabrina... and he made me tell him about what had happened to you."

"What!"

"Sabrina, I couldn't stop myself. I'm sorry."

"Mona, I told Solána not to tell Kisan, and now you've told Khaleeq! He's going to tell Kadeem, and we all know what they're going to do to Troy!" Sabrina fumed.

"Troy deserves it though," Solána mumbled.

"Solána!"

"Yes, he does, Sabrina! Wake up and realize that what he did to you was wrong! If The Williams want to make him pay, I don't see nothing wrong with that."

"They're going to kill him, Sol," Sabrina whispered in a terrified tone. "They're going to kill him."

"And so what?" Solána asked. "After what he did to you, death is too forgiving. Fuck that nigga."

"Damn," Monalisa remarked after Solána's cold statement.

"What?"

"You sound like... like a gangster," Monalisa informed her truthfully. "Not giving a fuck, saying it how it is..."

"She sounds like Kisan," Sabrina spoke up before sighing deeply. "I can't believe you told Khaleeq, Mona. But there's nothing I can do to change that now. I hear what both of you are saying, and I know how much you both hate Troy. What he did to me was evil, but I don't hate him. I just want him to get the help that he needs because for him to lash out like that shows that he needs help. Serious help. How can he get that help if he dies? I don't want The Williams to hurt him, so I'm going to warn him to get out of town or something. And I would really like it if you could both please respect my decision and not tell Kisan or Khaleeq what I plan to do. Just let me deal with this. Please."

"So she finally took your crazy ass back, huh?"

Kisan grinned at his best friend before taking a bite into his Chinese. Today, Kisan and Lucas were chopping it up together because this was Lucas's last weekend in Miami. He was moving back to New York in a few days.

"Yeah," Kisan said after chewing and swallowing his chow mein. "We're still working on things, but we're pretty much back together."

"That's good to hear, man," Lucas stated as he lifted his fork into his mouth.

"Are you absolutely sure that you want to move back to NYC?"

Lucas shook his head at his best friend, assuring him that he wanted to do this. It was all he had wanted to do for the longest, and at this point, he couldn't fight off his wishes. He was moving back where he belonged.

"Yeah, man, 100 percent," Lucas confirmed as he dropped his fork back into his takeout box. "But I'll make the effort to come back and forth to visit and shit. And of course, I expect you to do the same."

"For sure, nigga," Kisan promised with a smirk. "We both know if I don't come visit, you'll be a big cry baby."

"Yeah, yeah," Lucas dismissed his joke. "Says the nigga that was teary eyed when I first told him that I was leaving."

Kisan continued to smirk before chuckling lightly. "Whatever, man. Just make sure you don't get another best friend out there, or I'ma have to kill him."

Lucas smirked and lifted his fist up for Kisan to dap. "You know I'll never do you like that."

Kisan willingly dapped him back, and the men continued to eat while watching TV.

"You know what I've just realized," Kisan voiced. "You ain't met

Solána yet."

"Oh shit, you're right. I haven't. You definitely should set that up before I go. How can I not meet the girl that's got you whipped?"

Kisan's smirk grew wider, and he nodded in agreement, knowing that Lucas meeting Solána was a must before Lucas left for New York.

~

KHALEEQ EXHALED LIGHTLY before walking up the stairs and heading to where he knew April would be. It was time for him to do what he had set out to do. He had already made his mind up long ago, but telling Monalisa that he was doing it today meant that he was doing it today.

Straight after breaking up with April, his main focus was would be to call Kadeem and Kisan to let them know what Troy had done. What he had done to Sabrina was foul and there was no way that Kadeem would be willing to let him live another day on this earth. For now, Khaleeq wanted to handle things one at a time.

"April!" he shouted loudly as he stepped into their bedroom. Not seeing her in sight made him frown with dismay. "Where you at?"

"In here, love." Her gentle voice came from the bathroom, and Khaleeq sauntered toward the ajar door before pushing it open, only to find April beaming at him as she sat on the toilet seat.

"April, there's something I need to sa... What the fuck is that?" Khaleeq's eyes widened as he laid eyes on what she was holding in her hands.

A pregnancy test.

"I've been feeling so unwell ever since we got back from the DR, Leeq," she explained coolly. "And I've missed my period... So I went to buy a pregnancy test."

Khaleeq's heart began to race with anticipation as he awaited her to reveal what the results showed.

"We're pregnant, babe," she revealed as she lifted the test toward him to reveal two distinct red lines.

Positive.

CHAPTER 18

~ THE NEXT MORNING ~

"Kadeem, can you fuckin' calm down? I know this is difficu—"

"Difficult!" Kadeem yelled as he lunged his office telephone across the room. Both Khaleeq and Kisan moved out the way so it wouldn't hit them. "The girl I love has been battered by a stupid ass nigga that I knew I should have been gotten rid of!" He lifted his holder of pens and chucked it against the wall behind him, resulting in the ceramic holder to smash into pieces.

"Yo!" Kisan yelled at him, irritated at what he was doing. "Relax yourself before I make you relax."

"Fuck you," Kadeem snapped on him. "Fuck both of you! I don't care. I want that nigga dead right now. Right the fuck now!"

"And we're working on it," Kisan voiced tensely, feeling his frustrations mount with Kadeem's acting out. "But you need to fuckin' relax!" he shouted once again which was enough to make Kadeem stop acting crazy. "Troy wasn't at his old spot, but don't sweat, because we will find him. Like we find everyone who double crosses us, a'ight?"

Kadeem pinched the bridge of his nose, hoping it would ease down the stress that he was feeling. At this point, he just wanted to see

Sabrina. He was really pissed at her not telling him what Troy had done to her. The fact that he had to find out from his cousins and not her, completely angered him.

"I need to get the hell outta here," Kadeem mumbled before picking up his phone from his desk and placing it in his back pocket.

"Don't do anything stupid, Dee," Khaleeq advised lightly. "Just be patient. We will find him."

"Yeah, whatever," Kadeem fumed. "We need to find his ass quickly before I tear this whole city down."

"You tear this city down, and I tear you the fuck down," Kisan threatened simply. "Just cool it. I promise you on everything, we gon' make this nigga pay."

Kadeem said nothing in response to Kisan's words and gave his cousins one last irritated look before taking his leave, leaving Kisan and Khaleeq alone. Kisan looked over at Khaleeq only to see the stressed look on his face. He wasn't sure if it was just the stress from Troy being M.I.A. or something else, so he decided to ask.

"Leeq, you good?"

Khaleeq let out a deep breath before running his hand over his face. Then he walked over to the nearest couch and plopped himself onto it.

"April's pregnant."

Kisan's eyes widened with surprise as he kept both eyes on Khaleeq.

"Shit."

"Yeah," Khaleeq said plainly before repeating after him, "Shit."

"So what are you going to do?" Kisan queried, walking over to him and taking a seat next to him.

"I don't even know," he muttered in a bitter tone, cradling his mouth with his fingers. "But what I do know is that I need to tell Mona."

Khaleeq knew that telling Monalisa that April was pregnant was going to change everything. All the plans that they had made to be together were now officially ruined. Leaving April had seemed so much easier before, but now that she was carrying his child, everything had turned into a disaster.

Two hours later, Khaleeq arrived on Monalisa's doorstep with a heavy mind and a heavy heart. The conversation that he knew they needed to have was one that he didn't want to have at all. He'd rather be able to tell her that he was drawing up the papers for his divorce and working on moving out this week.

"You hungry, baby?" Monalisa questioned him warmly as she held his hand and led him toward her kitchen. "I could fix you something to eat real quick."

Khaleeq didn't respond straight away until they got into her kitchen and she broke away from him.

"Nah, I'm okay," he voiced calmly, watching as she walked over to her fridge and opened it, examining it carefully.

"You sure?" Her eyes remained sealed on her fridge, scanning her shelves for something to quickly whip up for him. "I could make you so—"

"Mona, April's pregnant," Khaleeq blurted out, cutting her off.

Monalisa froze in her stance, not sure if she was hearing things or if Khaleeq had really just dropped a bombshell on her.

"S-She's what?"

Khaleeq observed as Monalisa slowly turned to face him with a heartbroken expression fixed upon her pretty face.

"Pregnant, Mona," he repeated with a sigh. "I was about to break up with her when I found her in our bathroom... taking a pregnancy test."

Monalisa couldn't stop the water works even if she tried. They filled her lids and dropped out in seconds. Then they wouldn't stop.

"Mo, I'm so sor—"

"Don't come any nearer," she warned him firmly, watching as he took strides toward her. But she didn't want him to. She wanted him to stay far away from her. "Just stay away from me."

"Mo, please..." His saddened face could not be masked as he watched the tears fall out of her eyes. "Just let me explain."

"There's nothing to explain!" she yelled, her tears dropping faster.

"You got your wife pregnant. You were sleeping with her while sleeping with me."

"Nah, it wasn't like that, Mo. I hadn't touched her in weeks... except for on our honeymoon. A month ago. But that was only because I couldn't stop thinking about yo—"

"I don't want to hear it. Please leave my home."

"Mo!"

"Leave, Khaleeq!" she exclaimed, pointing to her door. "And don't come back!"

"I love you," he confessed wholeheartedly. "I'm not going to be able to stop loving you. April getting pregnant changes noth—"

"It changes everything," she interrupted him, giving him a nasty glare. "She's carrying your child, and you married her. Why I thought I could compete with her was honestly just me being delusional."

"I told you to tell me not to marry her," he reminded her, a frown forming on his lips. "Did you forget?"

"You should have been man enough to not go through with it. But you did, and I see that you always wanted her over me."

"Mo, please stop talking craz—"

"Don't come near me, Khaleeq!" she shouted once again, seeing him move toward her. "I'm serious!"

"Mo, I'm not letting you end us because of this little mishap."

"Mishap?" She gave him a crazy look. "Mishap? Khaleeq, she's pregnant! How the fuck is that a mishap?"

"Yo, quit on the yelling," he lightly snapped. "You know I don't like that shit."

"I don't give a fuck!" She pointed to the door once again. "Leave!"

"I'm not goin' anywhere until you listen to what I have to say."

"I don't care! I want you to go. I don't wanna listen to anything because you and I have nothing to talk about anymore, Khaleeq. You got April pregnant! *Pregnant!* So go and live happily ever after with your wife, and leave me the fuck alone. I don't want anything to do with you at all. I'm done! I lowkey wish you were dead because of all the problems you keep on giving me! My life was so much easier until you walked in!"

Khaleeq gave her a wide-eyed stare after her last statement, in disbelief that she had wished death on him. Monalisa instantly covered her mouth, completely shocked that she had said that to him.

"Damn," he remarked with sorrow. "That's how you feel?"

As much as she wanted to take it back, she couldn't bring herself to speak up again. She just watched the disappointment form on his attractive face and continued to get teary eyed.

"A'ight. I guess that's it then. We're done."

Khaleeq did not bother saying goodbye. He just turned away from her and headed out her door. Walking out her door with a heavy heart because he loved that woman with everything in him, but shit had just gotten too complicated. Way too complicated.

"I'M GOING to kill that nigga! I promise you, Sabrina! He's a dead man walking! And why the fuck didn't you call me and let me know what happened? Why you got me out here looking like a mothafuckin' fool? I'm supposed to protect you! Always! And you couldn't even let a nigga do that one job? I had to find out from my fucking cousins! Where are you? I came to your apartment and you wasn't there, so where the fuck are you? I need to see you, Sabrina! ASAP! Stop ignoring my calls and texts and hit me up!"

Sabrina hated how angry Kadeem was over the phone. His voicemail message had definitely told her that he knew about what had happened, and he was willing to make Troy pay regardless of how she felt about it. This was one of the reasons why she knew she had to tell Troy to get out of town. Hitting him up had felt strange, but she wasn't about to leave him in the dark when she knew that Kadeem was after him.

You need to leave town as soon as you can. People are after you because of what you did.

Send.

Sabrina still stood by how she felt the need to protect to Troy. Knowing that something had happened to him when she could have prevented it would forever haunt her which is why she freely reached out to him. He didn't reply on the day she sent the text. Instead, he hit her up the day after.

Troy: *Sab... I'm so sorry.*

Sabrina: *Are you out of town?*

Troy: *Yes.*

Sabrina: *Good.*

Troy: *I never meant to hurt you.*

Sabrina: *Well you did.*

Sabrina: *But I know you acted completely out of character which is why I know you need help, Troy.*

Troy: *Why haven't you called the cops on me?*

Sabrina: *Because I don't want that life for you. I just want to help you get the help you deserve. All your suicidal thoughts and now hitting me... were a cry for help. Troy you need help.*

Troy: *I know, I know... but seriously, Sab I'm so sorry for hurting you.*

Sabrina: *I know you are.*

Troy: *Can I see you?*

Sabrina: *We both know that's not a good idea.*

Troy: *I swear I won't try anything. You can even bring along one of your sisters if you don't trust me. I just need to apologize to you in person.*

Troy: *I'll send you my current address and you can make your mind up.*

Sabrina knew that going to see Troy wasn't the brightest idea. But going to see him with one of her sisters wasn't a good idea either because they wanted him dead for what he had done. She wanted to get Troy all the help he needed, but seeing him again was something that sent a chill down her spine.

Was seeing him after what he had done to her really a good idea?

YOUR TIME IS ALMOST UP, Dazhanae. I hope you're ready to tell him tomorrow.

April.

The fear and panic that Dazhanae currently felt were two feelings that she hadn't felt in a while. After giving April the DNA results, she was sure that she would no longer feel this way ever again. She had protected her precious lie and protected herself from Kisan. But unfortunately, that in itself was a lie. Her protection had been destroyed, and now she was left in a dreadful predicament.

I can't tell him. He's going to kill me. He's going to kill me, he's going to kill me, he's going to kill me!

Sweat formed on her forehead and upper lip as she contemplated more about the situation. There seemed to be no option out. All her thoughts were negative, telling herself that she couldn't fight this.

You need to kill her, Dazhanae. I can't kill her, I've never killed anyone before. Besides, she's too protected; she said so herself. Run away, maybe? Take Luciana and run as far as you can away from him. But he's so powerful, he has eyes everywhere... He'll find you before you've even found a new home. You need help; that's the only way you'll be able to get out of this. You need someone to help you out of this mess.

CHAPTER 19

"*L*u... baby, tell Daddy what you think of Solána?"

Luciana looked up from her book and gazed into her father's eyes through the rear-view mirror. Seeing the smile appear on her beautiful face at his mention of Solána made him smile back at her.

"I love her," Luciana admitted. "She's so prwetty and nice. I love Olivia too! She's so fun to play with."

"That's real good to hear, mama," Kisan replied as he kept his eyes on the road ahead. "Real good."

He was extremely grateful that the two women he loved in this life were getting along just fine with no problems. Luciana loved Solána, and Solána loved her just as much. They were bonding constantly, and that's all that he wanted, to see them bond and get along.

"I'ma see you tomorrow, a'ight, baby girl?" he told her as he kissed her forehead and stroked her soft curls. She gave him quick, sure head nods.

Kisan had arrived at Dazhanae's house after picking up Luciana from school, and now he was dropping her off.

"Bye, Dwaddy," Luciana concluded before running out of his arms toward her mother who stood on the front porch watching the pair.

Kisan gave Dazhanae a firm head nod before entering back inside his G-Wagon and heading to Solána's crib. He looked up at his rear-view mirror to see two black BMW's following behind at a safe distance. Knowing that he was being followed didn't faze him because he knew that his men were just doing their job.

But he hated it. He could protect himself; however, he understood the precautions his uncle Axel was taking ever since Khaleeq's shooting. They were still trying to find the culprit behind the shooting, and of course, the entire group responsible for wanting them dead in the first place. So far, they knew nothing, but Kisan knew that soon they would have the information that they required.

Once arriving at Solána's, he embraced his baby tightly into his arms and kept his head rested on her shoulder, resulting in Solána to giggle lightly at how affectionate he was being.

"Kisan, I know you love me and all, but damn, you're all up on me," she amusingly stated. "Give a girl some spaceeeeee."

"Shut the fuck up," he playfully snapped as his hands moved down her waist and squeezed her butt before spanking it. "I wanna be all up on my peanut."

"Kisan, ow, that hurt."

"As it should do," he whispered sexily as he spanked her once more, making her whimper. "You been a bad girl, teasing me with these lil' ass shorts of yours, so daddy's gon' spank that ass all day."

Solána continued to laugh happily, placing her arms around his tatted neck.

"Oh shit, I almost forgot," he announced, rubbing her butt. "I want you to meet Lucas before he leaves for NYC tomorrow night."

"Your best friend, Lucas?"

"Yup."

"Sounds good," she responded gladly. "When?"

"Later on tonight. I'ma text him to come through."

Solána nodded in agreement as she stared deeply into his pupils. Seeing the complete joy that was embedded within them as they embraced made her smile harder at him.

"Also, I want you to start getting yourself ready to move in with me, Sol." Her smile quickly faded. "As my girl, I want you living with m—"

"Excuse me?"

"Excuse the fuck what? You deaf now?" he snapped, loosening his grip around her. "Did I stutter?"

"I'm not moving in with you, Kisan," she voiced, pulling herself away from him. "And I'm not your girl."

"The fuck you just say to me? Of course you're my girl, Solána."

"I'm not," she repeated with a head shake. "I told you from the start that just because we were sleeping together again didn't mean that you and I were back in a relationship, Kisan. We're working on things; that's it."

"Have you actually lost your damn mind?" He gave her a nasty glare as she stepped back away from him. "You know damn well the day I came over here for Luciana's book was the day we got back together."

"No it wasn't!" she protested. "I told you, Kisan, you weren't just going to slide your way back as my man by using your dick to convince me."

"Well this dick has been doing a whole lot of convincing for the past few weeks!" he reminded her. "Stop talking crap; you know you my girl."

"I'm not, Kisan, and I really wish you would stop saying that. I also don't appreciate you trying to get me to move in with you like you own me or some shit."

"You've actually gone mad," he remarked with a scoff. "You've lost your damn mothafuckin' mind, Solána, but I promise you, I'm about to help you find it! You know who the fuck you belong to, so stop acting dumb. All the effort I've been showing you, letting you meet Luciana, this has all been part of our relationship getting back on track. And it's back on track!"

"Just because you let me meet Lu doesn't mean that we're back together. Just because you've been making an effort doesn't mean that we're back together. Just because you've been dicking me down every night doesn't mean we're back together! You hurt me, Kisan. You hurt me in the worst way possible, and you can't just click your fingers and expect me to forget about it."

"I thought we were past that shit though, Sol!"

"No, *you're* past it, Kisan! I'm not past shit!" she yelled furiously, pointing at herself.

"I really can't believe this shit right now," he remarked. "I can't believe the bullshit that's coming out of your mouth right now, Solána."

"It's not bullshit. I'm serious. We're not together."

"We are," he affirmed.

She simply shook her head with disagreement which only made his anger heighten.

"Stop shaking your head before I knock the shit outta you. We are together, Solána! The shit ain't up for mothafuckin' discussion!"

"Kisan, we are not in a relationship."

"Can you stop saying that shit!" he fumed, his chest heaving up and down "We are!"

"No we're not, Kisan. The sooner you realize that, the better."

"So you mean to tell me all the time we've spent together, all the affection I've showed you, all this dick I've given you whenever the fuck you wanted it, was all for nothing?" He gave her a scowl, still not believing the way she was acting right now.

Solána gave him a simple shrug before answering, "All I know is that I'm a single, independent young woman who has always been able to take care of herself, and I'll still be able to take care of myself regardless. I'm not moving in with you, and I'm not your girl, Kisan."

"I should really fuck you up right now," Kisan voiced with a light chuckle. "You really are playing these stupid mothafuckin' games with a nigga like me like I won't fuck you up?"

She shrugged at his threats and glared at him. "It is what it is, Kisan. I've said what I've needed to say and meant it."

"So if we're not together now, is there even any point of me still making a continuous effort with you? You ain't even giving a nigga a real chance! You've been giving me false hope this entire time!"

"Whatever you wanna do, you can do," she responded simply, and he hated how nonchalant she was being about the whole situation.

"So you don't want to move in with a nigga? I could get you a new big ass crib with all the closet space you gon' ever need, Solána. I'll even agree to get Olivia a mothafuckin' boyfriend that can fuck her all day in her playroom! We can have a bedroom the size of this whole house!"

"I'm good, love," she voiced nonchalantly, shrugging once again. "Enjoy."

He looked at her with resentment and anger, no longer in the mood to scream and shout at her. She had clearly made her mind up, and he was going to leave her to it. He wasn't about to play these childish ass games with her.

"Fuck you, Solána," he concluded coldly, cutting his eyes at her before heading toward her front door and leaving her home.

$\sim$

"Kadeem, son... I've been highly disappointed with your behavior for the past few months. You've been angry all the damn time and lashing out. I don't like it at all because it's not you, son."

Kadeem looked across the table at his father with shame, knowing how much of a fool he had been. He had acted out in the worse way from shooting soldiers at one of their warehouses and being spiteful to his cousins. His father wasn't even aware of the true damage that he had done.

"I'm sorry, Dad... Shit's just been so complicated lately," Kadeem explained and watched as a female waiter came to their table with a silver tray that had their drinks. "So damn complicated..."

Axel had rented out a seafood restaurant downtown Miami to spend some quality time with his son. He knew that he needed to have a serious talk with him and see where his head was at. He needed his son to act cool, especially with the threat that had been imposed on them due to Khaleeq's shooting.

"Because of that girl?" Axel questioned as the female waiter placed their drinks on the table. "Sabrina."

Kadeem simply nodded before taking his Sprite and sipping it. Sabrina was the only person that remained on his mind these days. The only woman that he could think about, especially with what had happened to her. All he wanted was Troy in a coffin.

"If she's been the cause of you lashing out and getting distracted, then I advise that you stay far away from her, son. A toxic relationship is not what you need right now."

"But I love her," Kadeem stated truthfully. "Yeah, shit between us has been really complicated, but we love each other. We've both done some hurtful shit to each other, but through it all, I know that I love her, Dad. That's the girl I'm going to marry someday."

Seeing the happiness that filled his son's eyes at the mention of Sabrina, made Axel smile back at him. His son had actually fallen in love with someone, and he was glad to witness it. All that was next was for him to witness his son walk down the aisle with the woman he loved.

Axel slowly lifted his glass to his lips as he spoke to Kadeem. "All I want is for my son to be happy but focused. If this girl makes you happy, then I say go for it all the way, but work on making your relationship with Sabrina stronger and better than before. You say you've both hurt each other; well stop hurting each other and start loving each other," Axel advised before taking a large gulp of his sparkling water.

"I hear you, Dad," Kadeem responded. "All I want to do is make her happy and of course be happy with her."

"That's the go... that's the goal," Axel stated with a light cough.

"You okay, Dad?" Kadeem noticed the uncomfortable look that had formed in his father's eyes.

"Just fine, son," Axel said before adding, "You should bring her 'round the house again so your mother and I can have a lovely dinne... dinn..." More coughs erupted out of Axel's mouth.

"Dad," Kadeem called out to his father with worry. "Are you sure you're good?"

"I a... am..." More loud coughs left Axel's lips, and Kadeem instantly waved the female waiter down.

"Water!" he shouted. "I need some water now! Yo, why the fuck are you still standing there like some fool? Get me water, bitch!"

The female waiter gave him a sneaky grin before dropping her silver tray and running back to the kitchen.

"What the fu... Dad!"

Kadeem looked on with horror as his father started coughing up blood. He raced out of his seat to tend to him, in the hopes that he could somehow get him to stop. How he planned to do that he had no clue.

"Dad! Where the fuck are you stupid servers at? Dad!"

The female waiter never returned with the water, and seconds later, Axel took his last breath before he collapsed onto the table.

CHAPTER 20

isan could not sleep. His annoyance had only increased during the night, and he tried to bury himself in some work, but that didn't help, because the only person he could think about was Solána and how pissed she had got him.

He didn't know where their relationship would go from here because she had freely let him walk out without even stopping him. It made Kisan question if she even cared about him anymore and if she had just been using him for dick and attention all this time.

Should we even still be together? I mean I love her, but... she drives me crazy. I don't know if she's healthy for a nigga like me. She gets me so worked u...

And that's why I'm so anti anti
Can't trust these bitches no cannot cannot, oh
and I, and I always keep some shooters on standby, standby, no

Kisan lifted his head off his pillow to look at his ringing phone on his lamp stand. He reached for his phone and looked as Kadeem's name appeared as the caller ID.

"Dee," he greeted him quietly. "What's u—"

Kadeem's sobs sounded through the phone. "They poisoned my mothafuckin' pops, Mace. Fuckin' poisoned him... Axel's dead!"

~

NEITHER OF THE men could believe it. It wasn't making any sense at all. How could the man who had raised them, guided them, and protected them be dead? At a time like this when they were heavy targets? At a time when they needed him the most?

Eva's loud wails from upstairs filled the mansion, and all Kadeem could do was wipe his tears as he sat on a sofa in the lounge. Kisan wanted to cry, but he didn't. He felt like his heart had been torn out of his chest. Axel had been the only father in his life, and to know that he was now gone... this was a heartbreak that Kisan hoped he would never have to experience until decades from now. He felt like a lost child, without any guidance or any comfort.

Khaleeq's tears were endless. He couldn't even look at any of his cousins. His eyesight was clouded with tears, and all he kept thinking was how did life get this sour? How did they end up like this?

"We're gonna find out who did this shit," Kisan promised, trying his hardest to not break into tears as he looked at his cousins. "I promise you both, the people that did this shit are not getting away with it. Not over my dead body."

Kadeem wiped the last of his tears before plucking up the courage to stare at Kisan in the eyes. He was afraid because of what he was about to reveal, but he knew that he had to do it. This was all his fault, and he needed to come clean.

"I know who did it," Kadeem revealed in a low, embarrassed tone.

Both Khaleeq and Kisan looked at him with deadly looks in their teary eyes. Kadeem took a deep breath before revealing it all.

How he had cooked up a plan out of anger to leave them and start up his own cartel. He went to seek the help of The Serbians because he knew how much clout they had on the outskirts of Miami, a small territory that The Williams didn't touch because they had no reason to. He wanted them to help him start up and make a cartel that would

158

be bigger than the Santora Cartel. But then after Khaleeq's shooting, he wanted out. The Serbians were trying to kill The Williams one by one, not help Kadeem build his own cartel. Now Kadeem realized how much a fool he had been and how greed had clouded his thoughts. The situation with Sabrina definitely played a part because he had been so angry about her cheating on him. Now his father was dead, and he was sorry more than ever.

Kisan stared blankly at his younger cousin, and Kadeem returned a fearful look, not sure what he was thinking.

"Kisan... say so—"

"I'm going to fuckin' kill you!" Kisan bellowed as he raced over to where Kadeem sat and gripped up his shirt, making him stand up in front of him. "You stupid, greedy idiot!"

Slap!

Kadeem's head instantly turned to the side, and his cheek burned with fire after Kisan's slap to his face. He didn't say anything or fight back; he just accepted the hard hit.

"This is all your mothafuckin' fault!"

Kadeem still didn't say anything and just took Kisan's yells whereas Khaleeq watched on with fury on his face. Fury at all the problems that Kadeem had caused them. All Kadeem remembered seeing was a violent look appear in Kisan's pupils before a hard blow pounded onto his face. Then Kisan's punches kept on coming, and Kadeem willingly took them all. Anything to mask the pain he was feeling from his father's death would do. So if Kisan wanted to give him an ass beating, then he would take it like a champ.

"Mace, stop!" Khaleeq shouted, rushing over to Kisan and pulling him away from Kadeem. "You'll kill him!"

"That's what I intend to fuckin' do!" Kisan spat as Khaleeq pulled him back. "Get the fuck off me!"

"Mace, chill," Khaleeq pleaded, still trying his hardest to hold down his arms and pull him away. "Now more than ever, we just need to stick together! We can't fight."

"This idiot didn't stick with us! He wanted to double cross us!"

"I know, I know," Khaleeq said gently. "But he's our cousin. He's family. We can't turn our back on him just because he did so to us. Mace, we need to work together and take these mothafuckers down. They killed our father! We gotta make them pay."

Kisan was finally able to shake Khaleeq off him and gave Kadeem a look of disgust. Seeing the blood that was oozing out of Kadeem's nose, his two swollen, red eyes and his bleeding cut lip, wasn't enough. Kisan badly wanted to hit him up some more; hit him until he beat the living lights out of him.

"He ain't no family of mine," he coldly spat.

~

How could he be such an idiot?

Kadeem's greed had cost them all, and now more than ever, Kisan loathed his younger cousin. He couldn't even stand to look at him without wanting to fuck him up, so he knew that the best thing for him to do would be to get home and get some sleep. He needed to cool off, and then hopefully in the morning, he could come up with a plan to sort this whole mess out.

Right now, he had his driver, Ethan, taking him back home. He couldn't drive, because he wasn't in the mood to, and he was so damn tired. It was almost midnight, and more than ever, his bed was calling him. He had been through so much pain today, from Solána and now losing his uncle. All he wanted to do was escape from it all, and sleeping was the only thing that could do that for him.

Solána was who he wanted other than his bed. He badly wanted to run home to her and cry in her arms. He wanted to smell her sweet vanilla scent and feel at peace in her arms. But doing that was impossible because of the way they had ended things a few hours ago. He considered calling her right now though, because more than ever, all he wanted was to hear her gentle voice.

And that's why I'm so anti anti
Can't trust these bitches no cannot cannot, oh
and I, and I always keep some shooters on standby, standby, no

Kisan lifted up his palm that held his vibrating phone only to see Dazhanae's name appear as the caller ID.

"Dazhanae? Why are you callin—"

"Kisan!" Dazhanae's cries and screams sounded through the phone, and he stared at his phone with dismay thinking that she was messing around right now. "Kisan, please! Help us!"

Us? His heart immediately raced with panic as he realized who *us* included. *Luciana.*

"What the fuck is go—"

"Kisa—"

"Listen up, little boy," a deep unfamiliar voice came on the line. "We've got your baby mama and your child here with guns to their heads. What we wan—"

"Who the fuck is this?"

"Shut up and listen up before I kill your precious little daughter," he said. "The code to the portrait safe. That's all we need, and we'll leave you and your family alone."

"Kisan, please!" Dazhanae's desperate voice came back on the line. "Just give him what he wants!"

"Listen to your baby mama, little boy."

"No! Who the fuck is this? Breaking into my daughter's house? Do you know who the fuck you're messing wit—"

"Kisan, please! He has a gun to Luciana's head! Kisan, please! She won't stop crying! I don't know the code or else I would have given him it already!"

The mention of a gun being plastered on Luciana's head made him feel paralyzed. He could never let anything happen to his child.

"The code to the safe!" the deep voice yelled. "Or I'm shooting your daughter first."

"Alright! Alright!" he shouted in defeat. "Just don't touch my kid, man. Please," he begged. "It's 23, 08, 81."

It was his mother's date of birth, something that Dazhanae didn't know, which is why she couldn't give it to whoever the fuck this man was. But one thing Kisan knew for certain was who was behind this stupid stunt. *Those stupid ass Serbians have broken into my daughter's house and touched her. I'm going to kill them all!*

After Kisan said the code, the call dropped, and he yelled out in anger as he chucked his phone against the car's front window. It almost hit his driver, and Ethan gave him a look of worry through the rear-view mirror.

"Is everything alrigh—"

"No! Nothing's fucking right! Get me the fuck to Dazhanae's now!"

Ethan did as he asked, speeding through the streets of Miami. Twenty minutes later, they had arrived, and Kisan didn't even wait for the car to stop before rushing out of the car.

He wasn't pissed about his safe being robbed. What he was pissed about was someone putting a gun to his daughter's head and he knew that that someone needed to die tonight.

"Luciana!"

Kisan shouted for his daughter, bursting through the house and looking for his child.

"Lu!" he yelled as he frantically rushed up the stairs. "Dazhanae!"

He burst into Luciana's bedroom, switched on the lights only to freeze in the doorway with bewilderment at how empty her room looked. And when he entered deeper and started examining drawers and wardrobes, he noticed all of her clothes were gone.

When he went to Dazhanae's room, the same thing had happened. All of her clothes were missing. Now confusion filled him as he wondered why all their stuff was gone? Had the robbers kidnapped them instead?

He rushed back downstairs to the living room only to see Luciana's portrait wide open, exposing the open safe. He got to it and saw that all the money was gone. All that remained was a single letter, and he picked it up, still filled with confusion. He quickly began to read it.

Dear Kisan,

I know by now you must have realized that my stuff and Luciana's stuff are all gone. And you must be so confused. There wasn't really a robbery. I staged it with the help of... let's just call them friends, to get the safe's code from you. I needed the money so that I could start a new life with Luciana away from you. You're never going to see us again. I didn't do this on purpose. I just needed to be far away from you. Especially now that someone's found out the truth. I know you're shocked and probably in disbelief at me taking Lu, but the truth is... she's not even yours. I cheated on you all those years ago with someone you know very well. It was my plan to take your money because I knew we needed whatever extra funds we could get so that we can start our new life together. Just me, Luciana, and him, together forever without you. The truth is, I named her after her dad. Lucas, your best friend, is her real dad. And we're going to be with him now. Goodbye, Kisan.

Tears had filled Kisan's eyes and were now falling out. Shock wasn't even the word he could use to describe how he felt. He could feel his heart breaking into tiny pieces, one by one which each breath that he took.

Ding!

He felt his phone vibrate in his back pocket, and when he brought it out, he looked down to see a text message from... *Lucas.*

Nigga, you never hit me up to meet Solána? Is everything cool?

Kisan felt his fury boil as he looked down at Lucas's text. How dare he text him after the stunt he had just pulled with Dazhanae?

Kisan: *I'm going to fucking kill you.*

Kisan: *I promise you, you a dead man tonight.*

Lucas's response was swift.

Lucas: *Kisan? What the hell is up with you?*

Kisan: *You know what the fuck is up! You stupid mothafucker!*

Kisan: *All this time you've been playing me! You and Dazhanae, together! You both are getting a bullet tonight when I find your asses. You can't hide from me. You of all people should know that shit.*

Lucas: *Kisan... seriously bro, what the hell are you talking about?*

Lucas: *I haven't seen or spoken to Dazhanae since I last saw Luciana.*

Lucas: *Which was last week.*

Kisan's confusion made an appearance again as his tears streamed out of his eyes.

Lucas: *I'm still in my crib. Come on man, you know this. My flight to NYC is tomorrow.*

Kisan didn't know what the hell was going on. This situation wasn't making any sense to him at all.

Lucas: *What the hell is going on man? Talk to me. Please?*

"Tʀʏ not to think about it, sweetheart. I know it's hard, but we don't want any stress on the baby," Teyana voiced sweetly as she stroked April's back. April revealing to her that she was pregnant had been the best news Teyana had received all week. Her son was finally having a child which meant that her first grandbaby was on the way.

"I can't believe he's dead though... This is horrible," she said with teary eyes.

"Horrible," Teyana whispered. She too had teary eyes.

They had just put Eva to sleep and were about to try to get some sleep themselves. But the news of Axel's death was devastating to say the least. April had lost her father-in-law, and Teyana had lost her brother-in-law, an important man in both their lives.

"But we need to move on and trust that the boys will handle this," Teyana explained as she gave April's back one last rub. "Let's see this baby as a ray of hope for what is to come."

April nodded in agreement before placing her hands on her flat stomach. She was only over four weeks pregnant, so no bump had formed yet. But that wasn't going to stop her from imagining that one was there. She couldn't wait for it to grow bigger in size.

"I'm just happy to be pregnant. Now Khaleeq can pay extra attention to me," she voiced. "And me alone."

Teyana gave her a wary look, and April instantly noticed it.

"What?"

"You alone, child?" Teyana asked, curious to know the meaning behind April's words.

"Yes," April confirmed with a firm nod as she continued to rub her flat belly. "Me, alone and no one else. After all, I'm who he loves, right?"

Teyana gave her a sure nod, not wanting to make her doubtful by revealing her son's secrets.

"Fuck that other bitch," April blurted out which made Teyana give her a shocked look.

"You knew?" Teyana asked, full of surprise at April's revelation.

"Of course I knew," April said defensively. "That's why I got pregnant."

Teyana continued to stare at her with shock, still not believing that April knew about Monalisa.

"How long have you've known?"

"I followed him the day before our wedding... and saw him go to her home. Then it all made sense. The coming home late, the lack of sex and attention..."

"And you still married him knowing?"

"Of course I did. I love him, and I'm not letting him go. And you telling me on the day of our wedding to hurry up and have your grandbabies, only confirmed that you knew too," April commented smugly. "So thanks for the advice, *mother-in-law*."

"He still loves her though. He's not gonna stop just because you're pregnant with his child."

"Then I guess I'm just gonna have to make him stop, aren't I?" She smiled to herself. "I'm gonna get rid of her. Simple as."

Teyana's face softened as she examined April's determined face once again. This was the woman who was carrying her son's child, so she knew that she needed to have her best interest at heart. Khaleeq not being in love with April was just something that Teyana was willing to overlook. The better woman was April and Teyana was willing to stand by her side.

"I'll help you," Teyana announced calmly. "Let's get rid of her together."

A NOTE FROM MISS JEN:

Part two is done already... wow, it feels like it was just yesterday when part one was put out. You guys have been messaging me every single day about part two, so I hope you're happy now... well you'll probably be upset because now you have to wait for part three lol! But don't worry. I promise it's on the way very soon! Dazhanae, Dazhanae, Dazhanae... wow, how could she be so cruel? But I'll tell you who shocked me the most in the book, April! And Khaleeq's mother, Teyana! I can't believe they're really about to work together to come for my good sis, Monalisa. But anyways, we'll just have to see what happens... I'm really worried about Kisan. Lord knows what he'll do now that he knows the truth. I know a few of you wanted Solána to date Cathan again, but guess what? He's got his book on the way soon, so don't worry. I promise you will get to read about his life, 'cause trust me it's juicy!

Please head over to my official website where you'll be able to see the visuals of all The Winters sisters/cousins and The Williams men: www.missjenesequa.com. My website also includes ALL the visuals from my previous works, so don't hesitate to go check it out! And make sure you join my readers group on Facebook to stay in touch with me and my upcoming releases: www.facebook.com/groups/missjensreaders. I'll be posting sneak peeks from the next part in my readers group, so make sure you're a part of it!

Thank you all so very much for the support; it is truly heart-warming.

Love From,

#TheFreakInTheBooks.

ABOUT THE AUTHOR

Miss Jenesequa is a best-selling African American Romance & Urban Fiction novelist. Her best-known works are 'Bad For My Thug', which debuted at #1 on the Amazon Women's Fiction Bestseller list, 'Loving My Miami Boss', 'He's A Savage But He Loves Me Like No Other' and 'Sex Ain't Better Than Love' which have all debuted top 5 on Amazon Bestseller lists.

Born and raised in London, UK where she always dreamed of becoming successful at anything She put her mind to. In 2013, she began writing full length novels and decided to publish some of her work online through Wattpad. The more she continued to notice how much people were enjoying her work, the more she continued to deliver. Royalty via Wattpad found Jenesequa and brought her on as a published author in 2015. Her novels are known for their powerful, convincing storylines and of course filled with drama, sex and passion. And they are definitely not for the faint-hearted. If you're eager and excited to read stories that are unique to any you've read before, then she's your woman.

Stay Connected

Miss Jenesequa's Reading Room

Feel free to connect personally with Miss Jenesequa at:
www.missjenesequa.com

Thank you so much for reading! Don't forget to leave a review on Amazon. I'd love to know what you thought about my novel. ♥

ALSO BY MISS JENESEQUA

Lustful Desires: Secrets, Sex & Lies

Sex Ain't Better Than Love (2 Book Series)

Luvin' Your Man: Tales Of A Side Chick

Down For My Baller (2 Book Series)

Bad For My Thug (3 Book Series)

Addicted To My Thug (3 Book Series)

Love Me Some You

The Thug & The Kingpin's Daughter (2 Book Series)

Loving My Miami Boss (3 Book Series)

Crazy Over You: The Love of a Carter Boss (2 Book Series)

Giving All My Love To A Brooklyn Street King (2 Book Series)

He's A Savage But He Loves Me Like No Other (3 Book Series)

Bad For My Gangsta

Royalty Publishing House is now accepting manuscripts from aspiring or experienced urban romance authors!

WHAT MAY PLACE YOU ABOVE THE REST:

Heroes who are the ultimate book bae: strong-willed, maybe a little rough around the edges but willing to risk it all for the woman he loves.

Heroines who are the ultimate match: the girl next door type, not perfect - has her faults but is still a decent person. One who is willing to risk it all for the man she loves.

The rest is up to you! Just be creative, think out of the box, keep it sexy and intriguing!

If you'd like to join the Royal family, send us the first 15K words (60 pages) of your completed manuscript to submissions@royaltypublishinghouse.com

LIKE OUR PAGE!

Be sure to <u>LIKE</u> our Royalty Publishing House page on Facebook!

CPSIA information can be obtained
at www.ICGtesting.com
Printed in the USA
LVHW04s0826140918
590145LV00016B/677/P

9 781722 305550